"I made you p... keep them."

"That's my Logan," Amy whispered. "Always doing the right thing. The honorable thing. That's how you got into this mess to begin with." She leaned in, her chest brushing his. "We both have a chance to get out of this. To get our lives back. All you have to do is sign."

He caught her wrists and pressed kisses to her palms. "I vowed to take care of you and love you every day of my life."

She stilled, her expression lifting. "And do you? Love me?"

"You were the best damn friend I'd ever had. I've always cared for you."

"That's not what I'm asking." She stepped closer, the heat in her eyes burning into him. "You said you swore to love me. What does that mean to you?"

"It means you have my loyalty. My fidelity and protection. And my support."

Her face fell. The spark in her eyes faded. "Those are all very important things," she said. "But what about your heart?"

Dear Reader,

I met a boy in college. A brawny, flirtatious one with a wide smile. He wore designer jeans, an expensive watch and spent way too much time on his hair. He enjoyed starting an argument and making me blush. He did everything he could to get me to look up from my books and give him attitude.

I thought he was ridiculous and told him so. I even rambled off a list of everything I disliked about him.

He just laughed and said, "Keep going."

That's how it started. But not how it ended. Jason became the best friend I'd ever had. He knew my shyness was debilitating. He coaxed me out of it. He persuaded me to join his kickboxing class, showed me how to hustle at pool and talked me into one more dance after closing time. The music would stop, the lights would go out and he'd just whisper, "Keep going."

Jason was a fearless boy. He would've grown into an extraordinary man. Only, he never had the chance.

In *The Rancher's Wife*, Logan Slade loses someone very important to him. His heart becomes hard, fills with regret and he finds it difficult to move on. It takes someone special to help him love again. To teach him to keep going.

Thank you for reading Logan's story.

April

THE
RANCHER'S
WIFE

———

APRIL ARRINGTON

HARLEQUIN®WESTERN ROMANCE®

Recycling programs
for this product may
not exist in your area.

ISBN-13: 978-0-373-75728-2

The Rancher's Wife

Copyright © 2016 by April Standard

Printed in U.S.A.

www.Harlequin.com

April Arrington grew up in a small Southern town and developed a love for movies and books at an early age. Emotionally moving stories have always held a special place in her heart. During the day, she enjoys sharing classic literature and popular fiction with students. At night, she spends her time writing stories of her own. April enjoys collecting pottery and soaking up the Georgia sun on her front porch. You can follow her on Twitter, @april_arrington.

Books by April Arrington

HARLEQUIN AMERICAN ROMANCE

Men of Raintree Ranch
Twins for the Bull Rider

Dedicated to Jason.

"Keep going."

Chapter One

Almost. Two syllables with so much promise and no damn reward. The most disappointing word in existence.

Logan Slade stifled a grimace and spun the ring on his left hand with his thumb. The silver band glinted with each twist. He eyed the nervous movement, willing it to stop. It was an absentminded habit. One he'd almost managed to quit.

His mouth twisted. *Almost…*

"We'll almost have snow," the white-haired man at his side chided again. "Yes, siree. Just needs to be a few degrees colder. They're predicting sleet tonight instead. Strange, huh? November ice in Georgia? Guess the angels left the fridge open." He laughed.

A shaft of frozen air abraded Logan's forearms and he clutched the door of Hartford Insurance Agency's lobby against the whipping wind. Crumpled leaves swept across the walkway outside in a violent flurry. Logan began to regret his impulse to jump up and assist the elderly man out. The chill pierced his skin but he kept his grip, willing the man to shrug into his coat a little faster.

"My Pearl loved the snow," the man mumbled. His

jubilant expression melted away. "We almost had some here last Christmas." Gnarled fingers struggled to fasten the top button at his neck.

"Here. Let me." Logan tucked his heel against the door and gingerly threaded the button through its hole.

"Almost…" the man whispered, his gray eyes lifting.

Logan stilled. It was impossible to count the regrets haunting the depths of his gaze. They pooled in the corners of his eyes, seeping into the crow's-feet and coating his white lashes.

Almost. Logan had almost not come today. Was no more than two thoughts away from calling the trip off when he finally twisted the key in the ignition and allowed his truck to haul him from his ranch.

And, after arriving, he'd almost left. Empty-handed, but with a heart crammed full of a thousand more regrets than he already carried.

Logan straightened, renewing his hold on the door. *Almost* be damned. He wasn't leaving until he did what he'd come here to do. What he should've done a long time ago.

He wasn't leaving until he saw his wife. And he wasn't leaving until she left with him.

The man's eyes still hovered on him. Logan summoned up a polite smile.

"Thank you, son," the elderly man said, shrugging further into his coat and edging out. "Yes, siree. Just a few degrees…"

The arctic blast receded as the door closed and Logan returned to his chair by the exit. He pressed his palm against the thick fold of papers stuffed inside the pocket of his jeans. They cracked under the pressure of his touch, shooting chills through him.

The massive grandfather clock in the corner sounded the five o'clock hour, doling out bellows and chimes. Each lilt of the bells pierced his ears and dropped into the hollow of his gut.

"How much longer do we have to sit here?"

Logan jerked his head to the side. The teenager beside him slumped further into a crumpled heap on the wide lobby chair. A thick hood obscured her face.

"Please sit up, Traci," he said.

"This is stupid." The hood shifted with her grumble. "Why can't we wait at her apartment?"

Logan shifted in his seat, heat spiking up his neck. "We're in public." He clenched his teeth, his knee bouncing with agitated jerks. "Sit up, please."

The hood dropped back. Emerald eyes flashed up at him. Eyes the same shade as those of her older sister, Amy. *His wife.*

Logan snatched in a breath. Dear God, Traci reminded him of Amy. Made it impossible for him to forget how much he missed her or how much he'd failed her. As a husband and a friend.

Amy had been his best friend long before she'd been his wife. That was how it should've remained. He'd never wanted to jeopardize their friendship by clouding it with lust. But that was exactly what he'd allowed to happen. When he found out she was pregnant, the only option he was willing to consider was marriage. And damned if that wasn't exactly what Amy had planned on.

"I can show you where her apartment is, you know?" Traci smiled. "It's not that far. Only five or ten miles."

Logan ducked his head and dragged a hand through his hair, the searing heat engulfing his face. He didn't need directions to Amy's apartment. He'd memorized her address four years ago. One day after she left.

He'd spent each morning counting the miles between them and each night adding more hours to her silent absence. The simple fact was, she'd never issued him an invitation to visit.

Logan had known better than to expect it. Amy had always been stubborn. Still, he'd hoped time would work its magic. Help her heal and bring her around to reaching out to him.

And she had finally reached out. But in a different way entirely.

Logan's fist clenched. His knuckles dug deep into the denim covering his thigh, driving a dent in the packet of papers filling his pocket. He wished he hadn't signed for them. Wished he hadn't taken the manila envelope from the mail carrier's hands, opened it and read them. Wished this ice storm would've changed direction and missed Georgia altogether.

Then, he wouldn't have been forced to leave Raintree and make the six-hour drive to Augusta. He could've continued to remain on the ranch, reminding himself why things were better left alone.

"We're waiting here," Logan muttered through stiff lips.

"But the apartment complex is right down the road." Traci perked up, straightening and sliding to the edge of her seat. "It's next door to a coffee shop and there's a rec room in the main hall that has a pool table. We could get a latte and shoot a round or two while we wait for her." Her slim hand latched on to his forearm, voice rising. "They have a sub place, too, if you're not in the mood for coffee." Her nose wrinkled. "It's different in the city. It's not like back at the ranch. Everything's right around the corner. You can find anything you want."

Yeah. He could find anything he wanted here. Anything except the friendship he'd once shared with Amy. The only place he had any hope of resurrecting that was back at their childhood home. At Raintree Ranch, the memories were rich. They grew out of the ground and wrapped around you on the wind.

"No," he said. "We're waiting for Amy here."

Amy. Logan's mouth tightened. *His wife. His best friend.* Alone. Hundreds of miles away from her family.

No doubt she could hold her own in a big city full of strangers. Otherwise, he never would've agreed to her decision to leave four years ago.

At the time, he'd thought it was for the best. A chance for her to experience life somewhere else. Shake the depression she'd fallen under after the loss of their daughter. Learn and grow. Mature into a woman who knew the value of honesty and loyalty. Then, she'd choose to come back. Only, she hadn't come back.

Logan sighed. He just needed to get Amy home. Back to her family. The sooner they returned to Raintree Ranch, the better.

"It's not a big deal," Traci continued. "Amy won't mind if we wait for her at the apartment. She told me I could use it whenever Mama and I visited. Even if she wasn't there." Her eyebrows rose. "It's better than sitting here—"

"I said, no."

"You heard that man. It's gonna sleet. The sign says they close at five and it's five," she stressed. "There's no one here but us now. She's not coming and if we're not going to her apartment, we're better off leaving without her. Before it sleets and we get stuck here. Let's head back now."

"I said no." Logan shot her a firm look. "Now, that's the end of it."

Traci released her death grip on his forearm and flopped back in an indignant heap. "I swear, if I miss Mama's turkey and dressing tomorrow, I'll never forgive you, Logan." Her lip curled. "Never."

Logan tensed and cast his eyes up to trace the popcorn patterned ceiling. *Teenagers.* Any other day Traci wouldn't utter two syllables strung together. Today, though, the endless chatter had begun the second the kid jumped into his truck insisting she take the trip with him. It had continued in a never-ending stream since.

Logan shot to his feet. "Wait here." Taking swift steps to the reception desk, he tossed over his shoulder. "Quietly."

A rough exhalation was her only response. *Thank God.*

"Excuse me, ma'am." He placed his hands flat on the reception desk to still the tremors running through them.

The young receptionist looked up, smiled and eased closer to the counter.

"Your daughter sure is talkative," she giggled. "I don't think she's drawn a breath in the last hour."

"She's not my daughter." Logan's throat tightened, a sharp pain ripping through his chest. "She's my sister-in-law."

"Oh." Her smile slipped. "I'm sorry. I just assumed—"

"I don't mean to be a pest but I was wondering if Amy Slade has come in yet?"

Her forehead scrunched, confusion clouding her features. "Amy Slade? You mean Ms. Johnson, right?"

Logan swallowed hard, the wad of papers in his pocket burning through his jeans.

He nodded, forcing out, "Johnson. Amy Johnson."

"Well, she had a lot of claims to document today. She was trying to squeeze in as many as she could before she left for vacation." She grimaced in apology. "I thought she'd be back by now but it looks like she may not make it in. I'm sorry. I know you've been waiting a long time."

"Can you give me her cell number?" His face flamed. "I'd like to give her a call. Let her know I'm here."

"Sure," she stated quietly. She held a business card out between pink nails. "I could…"

Johnson. Logan's hand halted in midair. There it was. Her maiden name. In bold, black ink stamped in the center. Plain print. Thick paper. Such a harmless item. But it cut to the bone.

"Sir?" Concern contorted the receptionist's features. "I could give her your number, if it's an emergency? Ask her to give you a call tonight? Or tomorrow?"

"No," he choked, ripping his hand away from the card.

He'd let four years of tomorrows slip by. He should've been here yesterday. His shoulders slumped. *Four years of yesterdays.*

"No, thank you," he repeated. "I'd like to wait a little longer."

A push of cold air swept in from the hallway, fluttering the papers on the desk. The receptionist glanced over her shoulder at the muffled clunk that followed.

"Back entrance," she said, rising from her seat. "That might be her. I'll go check."

Logan strode around the desk to the mouth of the hall.

"Please give me a moment, sir."

He drew to a halt at her raised hand and pleading expression. She cast anxious glances behind her.

"Just let me tell her you're here. Please?"

Logan managed a stiff nod. She dropped her hand and moved down the hall, disappearing into a room on the left.

His legs tensed and his torso pitched forward. *Wait.*

He glanced back at Traci still slouched in the lobby chair then found himself inching down the hall despite his polite promise. His ears strained to capture the receptionist's hushed tones and low words.

"…been here for hours. Very insistent on seeing you."

"Who is he? Is he filing a claim?"

Logan faltered, his breath catching. *Amy.* There was no mistaking her soft, questioning tone. His steps quickened, the tips of his fingers slipping inside his pocket and curling around the papers in a crushing hold.

"I don't think so. I think he might be…" Hesitancy coated the receptionist's words. "I think he's your—"

"Husband." Logan clamped his lips together and flexed his finger against his wedding ring.

He'd reached the threshold. The view of the room remained obscured by the receptionist. She swiveled to face him, hands twisting at her waist.

His earlier reminder to Traci returned. *We're in public.*

He issued a tight smile. "I apologize for not waiting. I didn't mean to rush you but it's important that I see her."

Floorboards creaked. That quiet voice returned. It drifted around the receptionist's tense frame. "It's okay, Kimberly."

The receptionist blinked and glanced back over her shoulder. "Would you like me to stay, Ms. Johnson?"

"No. You go ahead and start your holiday. I'll lock up."

The receptionist hovered briefly then nodded and slipped past Logan, the click of her heels fading.

A thousand thoughts had clamored in Logan's head on the ride up here. A million words had vibrated on the tip of his tongue as he drove. He'd sifted through each one, preserving or discarding them with precision until he'd carefully arranged a select few that were the most important. The ones that needed to be delivered first. Ones that would give him a fighting chance.

One glimpse of Amy and every one of them dissipated. Just as they always had.

Amy had been a pretty girl from the start. Eight years old to his twelve when she'd first arrived at Raintree, she'd been all daring smiles and impish expressions. At nineteen, she'd been beautiful. That shiny length of black hair, and tanned legs that seemed to stretch on forever.

Now, as a woman of twenty-four, she was breathtaking. Curves replaced the coltish angles and a relaxed strength resided in her lithe frame.

"Logan."

His attention shot to the lush curves of her mouth and the deep jade of her eyes. Both opened wider with surprise.

"I needed to…" His blood roared, his tongue clinging to the roof of his mouth.

Needed to see her. Touch her. Hold her.

Amy's expression cleared. She regained her composure and took slow steps toward him, stopping when the toes of her shiny heels were an inch from the scuffed toes of his boots.

At well over six feet, Logan found it rare that anyone met him on his level. Amy, however, never failed to do so. Wearing heels, her slender frame reached almost the exact same height, her gentle breaths dancing across his jaw.

"It's good to see you," she whispered.

It was the last thing he'd expected her to say.

She rested her palms loosely on his shoulders, her smooth cheek pressing gently against the stubble of his. Her sweet scent enfolded him and soothed his senses. He closed his eyes and breathed her in, sliding his hands over her back to draw her closer.

She felt the same. Soft and strong. Only, now, the mature curves of her body met the hard planes of his, filling each hollow and reminding him of exactly how much he'd missed.

How the hell had he ever managed to accept her decision to leave? Encouraged it, even? And why had he waited so long to come? When all he had to do—

"You look well," she said, drawing back.

She crossed the room to the other side of the desk and removed her jacket to hang it on the back of the chair. Smoothing a hand over the collar of her sweater, she adopted a welcoming stance. A patient countenance.

It wasn't the empty expression she'd had years ago after the loss of their daughter. Or the defeated one she'd shown for months after several failed attempts at getting pregnant again. And it was a far cry from the rebellious one she'd worn as a girl, intent on challenging him at every turn.

This was something different. This was worse. It was the professional posture a claims adjuster assumed with a client. The polite demeanor a woman assumed with a stranger.

Logan balled his fists at his sides, his chest tightening with the familiar sting of regret. He'd waited too long.

"What can I do for you, Logan?"

She continued running her fingers over the sweater's neckline. The movements remained small and graceful. Not erratic or anxious. Certainly not an action that should draw attention.

A flush bloomed on the skin of her neck. A fraction of an inch above the tips of her fingers. Her bare fingers.

Logan's eyes burned. This trip was a mistake. Like so many others. There was nothing left of their marriage to salvage here. He should walk away, get back in his truck and leave. It was the sane, sensible thing to do.

He jerked his head to the side but couldn't force his stare to follow. It clung to the small motions of her fingers, causing the pink shade on her neck to spread and deepen to a fiery shade of red.

Logan clenched his jaw. He'd already lost a child. Hell if he'd lose his best friend, too. The girl he remembered was still there. Buried beneath the sophisticated veneer. And he wasn't leaving without her.

Reaching deep into his pocket, Logan withdrew the thick wad of papers and tossed them onto the desk. They bounced, slid across the mahogany wood and drew to a precarious halt on the far edge.

"I'm here to bring you home."

LIES VARIED. Amy knew that. They could be as white as a consoling whisper. Or as dark as a secret never spoken. As a girl, she'd only lied to Logan once but it had been dark enough to follow her for years.

Amy curled her fingers tighter into the collar of her sweater and refused to look at the papers balancing on the edge of the desk. Instead, she focused on Logan, lingering over the dark depths of his eyes, the strong line of his jaw and the sensual curve of his mouth.

He hadn't changed much in the four years since she'd last seen him. His lean length was still as sculpted as ever. His broad chest and shoulders were just as wide and impressive. And the familiar attire of jeans, collared shirt and boots were still the same.

A deep rush of longing enveloped her, making her ache to reach out and wrap her arms around him. To draw him close and hold on. Just as she had so many times over the years as a friend and, eventually, as a lover.

Dear God, she'd missed him. Missed his smile, his strength. Even his tight-lipped frowns of disappointment. Most of which had been directed at her over the years.

Her stomach churned. Figured the one thing she'd always admired most about him was something she had never been able to possess as a girl. Something she'd always found so elusive and so foreign.

Honor. Logan lived and breathed it. Even when it cut deep.

Amy smiled, hoping the slight quiver of her mouth didn't show. "I told Mom on the phone that I'd drive home as soon as I got off work today. I promised I wouldn't miss Thanksgiving dinner this year and I won't. I'm already packed and—" she flicked her sleeve back and glanced at her wristwatch "—it's time to close up. I'm about to swing by my apartment, grab my bags and head out. There was no need for you to make such a long trip."

A muscle in his jaw jumped. His left hand moved, his thumb twisting the ring on his finger. The same one she'd slid there years ago when she was a selfish girl of nineteen. A girl who had lied and purposefully gotten pregnant with Logan's child, knowing his honor would demand he marry her.

The memory conjured up shame. It scorched a path from her soul through blood to muscle, then sizzled on the surface of her skin.

There were so many things she couldn't change. But one thing had changed. She was no longer that selfish girl. No longer reckless or relentless in her pursuit of Logan. Always pushing for more than friendship and stealing his freedom from him.

She'd ruined his life back then. Hurt him more than she'd ever hurt anyone, and she'd never hurt him that way again.

Amy squared her shoulders and wrapped her hands around the chair in front of her. *End this fast. Make it clean and painless.*

"It may have been a while since I've made the drive," she said, trying for a small laugh. "But I can manage to find my way back on my own."

The tight grooves marring Logan's face deepened.

She longed to reach up and smooth the lines away with her fingertips. Cup his jaw and press her forehead to his. She'd done it so many times over the years it had become second nature.

But things were different now. She wasn't that naive girl anymore.

Logan moved, taking long strides across the room to reach the desk. The dark waves of his hair weren't cut quite as short and the lines beside his mouth were deeper. But, the slight changes only enhanced his rough-hewn appeal. If possible, he was more handsome now, at twenty-eight, than he'd ever been.

"Your mom was worried," he said. "Betty knows it's a long drive and she's concerned you'll get caught in the weather." His mouth tightened. "I was worried, too. They're calling for sleet. Driving in ice is dangerous. Especially when you're not used to it."

"Maybe." Amy tossed her hair over her shoulder and straightened, firming her tone. "But it'll be a good experience for me. I need to get used to driving in extreme winter conditions."

Logan frowned. "Why?"

She smiled. A real one that untied the knot in her chest.

"I've accepted a job in Michigan. There's a new insurance branch opening in Detroit and I'll have a management position. That means higher pay and more opportunities for advancement." She shrugged. "The winters are a lot harsher up there. Wouldn't hurt to get a little taste of it now before I move in January."

"Michigan?" Logan's frown deepened, his voice strained. "That's damned far, Amy."

He cut his eyes to the window, remaining silent for

a moment. The wind outside strengthened and tumbled bits of trash across the parking lot. A tree branch scraped across the glass pane, its shrill squeak breaking the silence.

"You've stayed here longer than I thought you would." Logan faced her again. "You used to say you loved Raintree. That you never wanted to live anywhere else."

Amy forced her features to remain blank. The only thing she'd missed as much as Logan and her family over the past four years was Raintree Ranch. Her mother and her younger sister, Traci, came to Augusta to visit every summer, but it wasn't the same as being together at Raintree. Their childhood home had always been her safe haven.

Even now, Amy could feel the warmth of Raintree's spacious kitchen. See her mother flipping pancakes on a wide griddle and humming happy hymns over the stainless steel stove.

Having secured a position at Raintree as head chef, the widowed Betty had brought her two young daughters with her to the beautiful guest ranch. And Logan's family had welcomed them all from the moment their feet touched the dirt drive.

As a girl, Amy had spent thousands of hours racing across Raintree's green fields on her favorite stallions, Thunder and Lightning. She'd helped Logan deliver both foals on the same stormy day. Logan had laughed at her choice of names, but at the time it had seemed like fate to her tender heart.

It had always surprised her how far and fast she could ride across Raintree's acres and still have ground to cover. And the gallop back had always been just as exciting knowing Logan would be watching and waiting for her safe return. The endless acres, beautiful horses and interesting visitors had made Raintree Ranch her favorite place in the world.

Amy had never known a more peaceful place. Until her selfish actions changed everything.

"I said a lot of things back then," she stated. "When I wanted something."

She'd wanted Logan. Marriage. *A family.*

Amy swallowed hard. That dream was gone. Logan had never loved her the way she'd loved him. Pushing him into marriage had destroyed their friendship and complications from pregnancy had almost taken her life. They'd been told she'd probably never be able to get pregnant again. That had been proven in the barren months that followed.

Amy shook her head. "All of that was a long time ago."

"Four years," he said.

"Yes."

Logan spun and crossed the room. The planks of the hardwood floor vibrated beneath her feet as his heavy steps carried him to the window. His spine grew rigid and he shoved his hands into his pockets.

She'd never met a stronger, more dependable man. But her deceit and their broken marriage seemed to have dented his armor. Cracked his bravado. And their stillborn baby girl—

Amy's lungs burned, sharp pain searing in all directions. That dark day had seemed like retribution. A justifiable punishment for her grievous sin.

Amy curled her toes and looked down at her shoes. She'd refused to give up on her dream of being a mother, though. But several failed attempts had forced her to finally accept that it was never meant to be.

She raised her head and straightened. That was all in the past. She'd moved on since then. She no longer mistook her admiration for Logan as love and she had let go of her dream of becoming a mother. All she wanted was to proceed with her respectable new life and continue giving Logan back his.

"The move to Michigan is why I decided to come home for the holidays this year," she said, working the words through her constricted throat. "I'm using some vacation time I have saved up to visit the ranch for a few weeks, see everyone and—"

"Say goodbye?"

Logan's accusing rasp shot across the room. He turned, yanked his hands from his pockets and rubbed them over his denim-clad thighs. The action seemed nervous and hesitant. Both emotions uncharacteristic of him.

"You sure are making a lot of decisions for everyone else," he said. "Doing a lot of assuming. As usual."

Amy rolled her lips and bit hard, a spark of anger lighting in her chest. One she hadn't felt in years. A product of the impulsive nature she'd worked so hard to shed.

Logan's dark eyes roved over her face, peering deep. He nodded toward the papers on the desk. "You gonna look at those?"

She held his sharp gaze, tensing and tempering her tone. "Later."

"Now's as good a time as any."

"I know what they are," she forced out.

The corner of Logan's mouth lifted. "I don't think you do. Take a look."

"You came all this way to boss me around?" Amy wrapped her fingers tighter around the chair. She tried to stop. She really did. But the words kept spewing. "I'm not a little girl anymore, Logan. You can't stroll into my life, toss orders about and demand I do things your way. Matter of fact, that never worked out for you back then, either, did it?"

"No, it didn't." Logan crossed the room, leaning into his palms on the desk and drawing close. "But it can work this time with the right persuasion."

Amy hissed and lifted her chin. "You think so?"

"I know so." A broad smile broke out across his lean cheeks, warming his expression. Logan lifted his hand, the blunt end of his finger smoothing over the tight line of her mouth. "There's my girl," he whispered. "I miss you, Amy. I miss *us.*"

Amy sagged against the chair, shoulders dropping. "Us fighting?" She shook her head. "Because that's all we're good at anymore."

His big palm cradled her jaw, calloused thumb sweeping gently over her cheek. "We're good at a lot more than that. We just need to work at it. Do things right this time."

Amy drew back, slipping away from his touch. "No. That's not why I'm coming home. And I don't plan on staying permanently. You already knew that." She nudged the papers with her fingertip. "That's why you signed these."

His eyebrows rose. "Did I?"

"Good Lord, I'm glad you're here."

Traci rushed into the room, sweeping past Logan

and barreling into Amy's middle. Grateful for the distraction, Amy wrapped her arms tight around her sister's waist. The bulk of Traci's coat made it difficult to pull her close.

"We've been waiting out there for hours," Traci mumbled against her neck. "It's cold, I'm bored and Logan refused to go anywhere. He wouldn't do anything but sit there and wait."

Traci's frantic whisper tickled her ear. Amy laughed, drawing back to say, "Why did you ride out here anyway? You knew I was coming home today."

Traci shrugged, stepping back and tugging at her hood. "You know Mama always starts cooking the night before Thanksgiving. If I'd stayed home, I'd have had to peel all the sweet potatoes for the soufflés." She curled her lip. "A girl can get carpal tunnel doing that." Her fingers picked at the cuffs of her jacket. "And I missed you." She shrugged. "Besides, there were too many people stuffed in that house. I needed to get out of there for a little while."

Amy smiled. "I take it Raintree's packed for the holidays, as usual."

"Oh, you don't know the half of it. I spend one summer visiting you in Augusta and munchkins invade while I'm gone." Traci shook her head. "When I got back to the ranch last August, six-year-old twins were tearing up the place."

"Twins?"

"Yeah," Traci said. "Dominic married their aunt last fall. They're seven now and I swear those boys got wilder. You'll see what I mean."

Dominic, Logan's younger brother, had been Amy's friend the moment she'd arrived at Raintree all those years ago. She couldn't imagine Dominic getting married and settling down. He was a nomadic bull rider, living in the moment and always searching out adventure.

"Dominic got married?" Amy glanced at Logan for confirmation.

Logan nodded, a small smile appearing. "He came home for good last year and he's happier than I've ever seen him." His smile slipped. "You've missed a lot."

Amy tensed, looking away from the sad shadows in Logan's dark eyes.

"We're really glad you're coming home for a visit," Traci said, squeezing Amy's arm. "It'll be nice for us all to be together again." She withdrew, moving around the desk to tug at Logan's elbow. "Can we start back now?"

"Soon." Logan nudged Traci toward the door. "Go on out and warm up the truck. We'll swing by Amy's, load up her bags, then head out."

Amy watched Traci leave then cocked her head at Logan. "Who's doing the assuming now?" she asked. "I never said I was riding back with you."

"No. You didn't." Logan walked to the door. "But I promised Betty I'd get you home safely, and I always keep my promises. Plus, your sister's been looking forward to catching up with you and there's no way I'm letting the two of you ride back alone in this weather. We'll follow you back to your place, get your stuff and you'll ride back with me. So lock up and meet us out front."

He left, leaving her glaring at the empty doorway. Amy huffed. It looked like Logan was getting his way again. At least, for the moment.

She firmed her mouth. Her plans hadn't changed. Not really. She'd accepted the new job and was moving to Detroit. Just as intended.

This trip home would still serve its purpose. She'd spend some time making amends, visit with family and find a gentle way to break the news of her move to her mother. Then, she'd move on to a new life and a fresh start.

It didn't matter what mode of transportation she took to the ranch. The path she'd follow would still be the same and her ticket to a new life was now in her possession.

Relaxing, Amy glanced down at the folded papers balancing on the corner of the desk, their ivory shade a stark contrast to the deep tones of the wood. She retrieved them, unfolded the pages, and slid her thumb over the bold heading.

Divorce Settlement Agreement.

She scanned the papers, each glimpse of blank space tightening her chest to the point of pain. Her fingers flipped up the corner of each page with a more violent flourish than the one before.

"If you're looking for my signature, you're not gonna find it."

Her head shot up. Logan stood in the doorway, his wide shoulders and lean length obscuring the exit. His grin widened into a firm curve, sparking his dark eyes with intent.

"Not now. Not ever," he said. "I never break my word."

Amy's breath caught. This was the Logan she knew. A bold, decisive man. One who never faltered once his mind was set on something.

He stepped into the hallway, tossing over his shoulder. "Go on and lock up. We need to start back soon. Before the storm hits."

The papers cracked in Amy's hand, crimping into a wrinkled heap before she dropped them to the desk. She stared ahead blankly, listening to the heavy tread of Logan's boots and the bell chiming on his exit.

The room was empty, her rapid breathing the only sound. Amy lifted her hand and slipped her fingers beneath the collar of her sweater to tug the silver necklace out. It dug into the back of her neck as she threaded her finger through the ring hanging from it. The weight of the silver band was familiar and comforting.

She squeezed her eyes shut. Only a few minutes with Logan and she'd reverted to old sins. She'd lost control, lashed out and goaded him into action.

The dig of the necklace turned painful, her finger straining to reclaim the ring. Amy gritted her teeth, slid the ring off her finger and shoved the necklace back beneath the cover of her sweater.

There was no way she was slipping back into old habits. Always trailing after Logan, begging for whatever attention he deigned to throw her way. What she'd felt for him all those years ago had been exactly what he'd called it. Ill-begotten hero worship. Nothing but a young girl's ridiculous fantasy. Something cynical– Logan would never deliver.

No. She'd come too far and worked hard to change. No way would she ever be that selfish girl again. She'd gotten over her obsession with him long ago.

Amy jerked open a drawer, yanked out her purse and shoved the wad of papers deep inside. This wasn't ending here. Like it or not, Logan was signing that agreement. And they were both going to shed the past and begin new lives.

She made her way through the lobby, flicked off

the lights and hovered by the window. The gray clouds grew thicker and the furious sweep of leaves through the parking lot whispered to a halt. Small white pellets plummeted from the sky in scattered patterns, slamming into the concrete and pinging against the glass pane.

Logan stood at the foot of his truck. Eyes fixed on hers, he crossed his muscular arms over his broad chest and leaned back against the tailgate. He didn't shiver or waver. Just stood there. A solid pillar of heat in the freezing onslaught of ice, not heeding its vicious bite.

Amy clenched her jaw. A sharp ache throbbed in her head at the tight press of her teeth. There was no need to rush. No need to try to outrun the storm. It had already hit.

Chapter Two

He'd come on too strong. Had pushed Amy too hard.

Logan shifted to a more comfortable position in the truck's cab and eased his foot off the accelerator. He glanced to his right, finding Amy in the same position she'd adopted an hour ago. Perfect poise, legs crossed at the ankles and eyes straight ahead. Her hands shook in her lap.

"Cold?" He stretched over to cut the heat up and angle the vent toward her.

"No. I'm fine, thanks."

She didn't look it. The closer they got to the ranch, the tenser she became.

"How much longer?" Traci asked from the backseat, removing her earbuds. "I'm getting stiff."

Traci rearranged her long length in the back of the cab, stretching her legs out to prop her boots on the console. Logan's mouth twitched at the sight of the muddied heels. A few clumps of dirt dropped from them, tumbling into the front seat by his jean-clad thigh.

He eyed her in the rearview mirror. "You got two floorboards back there, Traci."

"And a lotta leg," she drawled, raising her voice

above the deep throb of music from her cell phone. "I'm starving. We haven't missed dinner, have we?"

Logan shook his head. "Nope. We're right on time. Not much farther now."

Traci stuck the earbuds back in, settled against the seat and closed her eyes.

Logan faced the road again and they traveled in silence for a couple of miles before he glanced at Amy. The brash glow of the low-hanging sun flooded the cab and highlighted the pinstripes in her pantsuit. Her black hair was pulled up, giving him a clear view of her pale cheeks and blank expression.

Logan opened his mouth to speak but shut it quickly. He used to be able to talk to Amy about anything. Never even gave a thought to what he would say. Knew she'd be as eager for his thoughts as he'd always been for hers. But over the past twenty-four hours, he'd discovered that even though they were no longer separated by miles of road, a distance still remained between them. One he had no idea how to cross.

"Is dinner still at six?" Amy's green eyes flicked to the clock on the dashboard.

"Yeah. Betty runs a tight ship." It was almost 5:30 p.m. They'd cut it close. "We'll make it."

Barely. Despite his best attempts last night, they'd been unable to start home before the storm hit. Instead, the ice fell fast once they'd arrived at Amy's apartment and by the time he'd loaded Amy's bags in his truck, the roads were too slick to drive on. They decided it would be best to spend the night and start back in the morning after the ice began to melt. Traci had slept in the guest room and Logan had slept on the living room couch.

He winced and rubbed the kink in the back of his

neck. Or better yet, he'd tried his damnedest to sleep. It'd been hard to do with his legs dangling off one end of the sofa and his head the other. It didn't help matters that Amy's bedroom had been only a few feet away. He'd heard the rustle of sheets every time she'd tossed and turned. Apparently, she hadn't been able to sleep either.

He rolled his shoulders and tightened his hold on the steering wheel. At least they were almost home now rather than holed up in that suffocating apartment. It'd been obvious that Amy had already begun preparing for her move to Michigan. The stacks of boxes lining the living room walls had glared at him from the moment he'd entered. He'd done his best to ignore them but they'd loomed over him all night.

Logan's mouth twisted. No wonder sleep had eluded him. He hated this. Hated how quickly he'd become fixated on Amy again. How every thought running through his mind centered on her and excluded common sense. It made him feel weak. Vulnerable.

"Tell me about Dominic."

He turned his head to find Amy studying him. Those emerald eyes traveled slowly over his face and lingered on his mouth, warming his cheeks. Her lips trembled slightly.

She looked away, asking, "Who did he marry?"

"Her name's Cissy. He met her one night on his way back to Raintree. She was stranded by the side of the road with her nephews."

"Are those the twins Traci mentioned?"

He nodded. "Cissy's sister died early last year and the twins' father didn't want them. Cissy took the boys in but had a hard time providing for them. Dom brought the three of them to the ranch and we set her up with a job." A smile stretched his cheeks. "Dom fell hard for her. He loves those boys, too." He released a low laugh. "We all do. They're great kids, Amy. You'll love 'em. And Dom and Cissy are expecting—"

Logan bit his lip, cutting off his words. *Babies. Twin girls.* Nausea flooded his gut. He couldn't say either of those things to Amy. Could barely say them out loud himself.

Red blotches broke out on Amy's neck, marring her clear skin. She smoothed her hands over her blouse and sat straighter in the passenger seat. "I'm happy for him," she whispered.

She would be. When she'd first arrived at Raintree, Logan recognized right off that Amy shared the same wild streak as Dominic. It hadn't taken long for Amy to begin regarding Dominic as a brother and Dominic was equally fond of Amy.

Logan frowned. He'd always been pleased with Amy's close connection with Dominic but after his own friendship with Amy eroded, Logan found himself envious of her bond with his younger brother. Which was ridiculous. More of the irrational behavior Amy inspired in him.

"I called Dom last night," Logan said. "Asked him to let everyone know we were running behind. He said Betty was excited to see you. Said she couldn't stop smiling."

Amy tucked a strand of raven hair back into her top-knot. "I'm looking forward to seeing her, too. It'll be a good visit."

Logan glanced in the rearview mirror at Traci. She bent deeper over the cell phone in her hands and her fingers flew over the screen. Her music blared, the rhythmic bass pumping past the earbuds.

"Betty never mentioned anything to me about you moving to Michigan," he murmured. "You haven't told her your plans, have you?"

"Not yet." Amy twisted her hands in her lap. "But I will. There's plenty of time. I don't want to upset her at Thanksgiving."

He scoffed. "You think Christmas would be a better occasion?"

"No." She sighed. "But I couldn't bring myself to tell her over the phone. I will, though. When the time's right."

"Augusta is far enough. Michigan will feel like the other side of the world to her. You're gonna break her heart, Amy," he said, ignoring the tightness in his chest. He eyed Traci again. "Your sister's, too."

"They'll understand. They'll be happy for me."

"Knowing you're thinking of moving clear across the country won't make them happy." Logan grimaced. It sure didn't sit well with him. "No one that cares about you would be happy hearing that."

"What would you have me do, Logan?" Amy glanced over her shoulder at her sister before whispering, "Stay in limbo with you forever? The opportunity came and I took it. I have to move on at some point. We both do."

Her argument was sane and sensible. The kind he should agree with and understand. But he couldn't bring himself to accept it.

Logan palmed the steering wheel roughly and took a right turn onto the long dirt drive of Raintree Ranch. He lifted his foot from the pedal as the truck dipped into a pothole, sloshing muddy water against the sides of the cab. Fragmented patches of white speckled Raintree's sprawling fields. The late-afternoon sun that had melted most of the ice hung low on the horizon and night loomed closer with every minute.

Amy's pants legs rustled as she sat taller, craning her neck and looking out at their surroundings. Logan took the next turn through a gated entrance and she braced her hands on the dash, swiveling to glance over her shoulder at Raintree's wooden sign as they passed. The sweet scent of her shampoo released with her movements, lingering around him and making him ache.

They traveled past the large stables, barn and paddocks lined with white fencing and the multi-storied main house emerged into view. Logan smiled. The white columns and wide front porch were already adorned with garlands, wreaths and bows for the holidays. Betty must have decided to decorate early for Amy's return.

A tender expression crossed Amy's features. Logan's chest warmed. No matter what she said, Amy had missed Raintree. Her longing for their childhood home showed in every sweet curve of her face.

"It still looks the same," she said.

The gentle look in her eyes faded as the truck drew closer to the house. Her mouth tightened. She eased back in the passenger seat, shoulders sagging.

"Nothing's changed." Amy trailed her hands away from the dashboard and dropped them in her lap, fingers twisting together.

A heaviness settled in Logan's arms. "Yes, it has. Everything has been different since you left. For all of us." He covered her smaller hands with his palm and squeezed. "Please think this move over. Before you make a final decision."

She slid away from his touch. "The decision's already been made." Her voice lowered to a whisper. "It's for the best."

"Amy—"

"The twins are out," Traci shouted over her music, perking up and dragging her feet from the console.

Logan released a harsh sigh, bringing the truck to a halt and removing the keys from the ignition. Two blond boys scrambled over the ground at the end of the drive, gathering up what was left of the sleet and packing it into muddy balls.

"Hide everything you value and get your armor on, Amy," Traci said, yanking out her earbuds and shoving them along with her cell phone into her bag.

"Are they that bad?" Amy asked, a hesitant smile peeking through her tight expression.

Logan grinned. "Nah. They're just being boys."

"Yeah, right," Traci drawled. "Tell me that the next time they break my phone. Or take my bras and use them for slingshots. Or draw plans for their fort on my homework—"

"All right, Traci." He laughed, muscles relaxing. "I know they've done you wrong a time or two but they do it with love."

Traci harrumphed and shoved her door open.

"That's one warped way to look at it," she grumbled good-naturedly, jumping out and taking swift strides up the dirt drive.

The boys noticed Traci approaching and stilled. A huddle, quick whisper and nod later, they advanced, surrounding her and pelting her with their icy bundles.

"Stop it, squirts," Traci squealed, "or I'll smooch you into oblivion."

Traci swooped down with open arms, bag flopping over one shoulder, and chased them. One twin escaped but she caught the other, scooping up the wriggling boy and plastering noisy kisses all over his face.

"Yuck!" The escapee ran several feet across the mud and jerked to a halt at Logan's open door. He scowled, jabbing a dirty finger in Traci's direction. "Look what Traci's doing to Jayden, Uncle Logan. Tell her to stop."

Logan stifled a laugh. Leave it to Kayden. He was always the first to point the finger of blame.

"Come on, now," Logan said. "You can't go on the attack, then cry for help. Don't dish it out if you can't take it."

"I ain't did no dishing," Kayden argued. He paused, forehead scrunching before saying, "I *didn't* do *any* dishing."

"That sounds better," Logan praised.

Kayden nodded. "Aunt Cissy don't like us using no double negatives." He climbed onto the truck's running board and leaned into his hands on Logan's thigh. "Anyways, I ain't did no dishing. We were just throwing snowballs."

"There's no snow out here, buddy." Logan ruffled his golden hair. "Y'all were throwing ice."

"So." Kayden shrugged. "It's white."

"Unlike a friendly snowball, ice hurts and I'm sure Traci felt a twinge or two. Both of you owe her an apology."

"Yes, sir." Kayden rolled his eyes, the blue pools skimming over Logan then narrowing on Amy. "Is that her?"

Logan turned, absorbing the warm look Amy directed at Kayden, and smiled. "Yeah. This is your aunt Amy."

Amy frowned but quickly adopted a polite smile when Kayden leaned in for a closer look at her.

Logan helped Kayden jump from the running board back to the ground. "Why don't you go around and introduce yourself properly?"

Kayden took off, his blond head bobbing out of view as he rounded the front of the truck.

"It's not a good idea introducing me as their aunt, Logan." Amy unbuckled her seat belt. It snapped back with a clang. "I'm leaving for good soon."

"Maybe." Logan met her hard stare with one of his own. "But you're here now."

She shook her head, grabbed her purse and climbed out of the truck. Logan followed, strolling to the other side of the truck to find Kayden tipping his head back and staring up at Amy.

"Gahlee, you're tall," Kayden said, mouth hanging open.

Amy's grin faltered as she teetered, her high heels sinking into the mud of the driveway. Logan stifled a laugh. The combination of melted ice and dirt had turned the path into slick mush. She yanked against it, attempting to jerk her shoes free, but the sludge won out.

Kayden stepped closer, studying her sinking shoes, then observing the rest of her. He blushed and stuck out dirty fingers. "I'm Kayden. And that's my brother, Jayden, over there. Good to meet 'cha."

Amy lowered with care, braced with one palm against the truck for balance and shook his hand. "It's very nice to meet you, too, Kayden."

"Boys," a deep voice called.

They all turned. Dominic ambled down the wide front porch steps of the main house and crossed the lawn toward them.

"Uh-oh." Kayden smirked.

He tore off toward the house, Jayden and Traci following. Dominic swept the boys against his thighs as they passed, kissing their heads and shooing them toward the porch with a pat on the butt.

Logan held Amy's elbow and helped her regain her balance. "You gonna ditch those shoes now?"

"No need."

She steadied herself by holding his forearms and yanked her heels from the suck of the mud. They broke free with a deep slosh. She lifted onto her toes, released her grip on his arms and straightened her purse strap on her shoulder.

"Well, I'll be damned," Dominic drawled, smiling wide and knuckling his Stetson higher on his brow. He strutted over, landing a heavy pat on Logan's back, then edging past him. "My partner in crime has returned."

Dominic wrapped his burly arms around Amy's waist, lifting her in a tight hug and spinning in a wide circle. She laughed, pure contentment shining on her face and eyes welling with happy tears. Logan savored the sight briefly then shoved his fists in his pockets and looked away.

"It's about time your butt moseyed back, kid," Dominic murmured. "Where the hell you been?"

"Around." She struggled to catch her breath.

"I've missed you." Dominic leaned back and studied her. "We've all missed you."

Logan's skin tingled under the weight of Dominic's

stare. He glanced over, eyes locking with his younger brother's.

"Haven't we?" Dominic asked.

Logan nodded, dragging a hand from his pocket and kneading the back of his neck. That kink was back, the pain streaking from the base of his skull down between his shoulder blades.

Amy cleared her throat, tapping Dominic's ankles with the toes of her shoes. "You can put me down now."

Dominic's lip curled, his tone teasing. "Don't know if I should. Doubt you'll make it to the house in those city-girl contraptions." He frowned at Logan. "You let her run around in these things?"

Logan opened his mouth but Amy beat him to it.

"He doesn't need to *let* me do anything." She popped her knuckles against Dominic's shoulder. "I do what I want when I please. Now, put me down."

Dominic chuckled. "Yep." He nodded with pleasure at Logan. "This is damn sure our girl you brought back with you."

"Almost as good as new," Logan said, voice catching.

Amy's cheeks flamed cherry-red and she shoved harder at Dominic's broad shoulder until he lowered her to the ground. Logan stepped forward, keeping a close hold on her elbow until she steadied on the mud and shrugged away his touch.

Amy nudged the bobby pins holding her updo into a more secure position and asked, "Were those your two misfits I saw earlier?"

The pride in Dominic's face was unmistakable. "Yep. Those are my boys. I adopted them last year after I married their aunt. Wished you'd been here for it, Ames."

He smiled. "Can't wait for you to meet my wife. I know you'll love Cissy as much as I do. And we're expecti—"

"That's enough for now, Dom." Logan's throat tightened at the quiver in Amy's chin. "It's been a long drive back. Let her rest before you yap her ear off."

Dominic nodded, his smile dimming. "Sun's dropping." He waved a tanned hand toward the horizon. "It'll be dark soon. 'Bout time I started rounding up the horses."

"I'll help," Amy said.

She squeezed Dominic's arm and brushed between them, making her way toward the paddocks grouped near the massive stable.

Dominic crossed to Logan's side, watching Amy's slow progress across the field. "How is she?"

"Better than she was four years ago," Logan said, trying to ignore the hollow in his gut at the memories assailing him. Amy, pale and unconscious, lying in a hospital bed while he sat by her side praying she'd wake up. His relief at her pulling through had been short-lived. After losing their daughter, she'd become a shadow of her former self. Each failed effort at becoming pregnant again had caused her to grow more listless and depressed over the following months.

Logan studied Amy's careful steps toward the paddock. "She seems physically healthy at least but she's still not herself."

The sun dipped sharply and an orange glow of light flooded the fields, silhouetting Amy's lithe figure. The outline of her curvy form turned black, becoming a stark contrast to the fiery light bathing the landscape.

"Y'all made any decisions about the future?" Dominic asked.

Logan sighed. "Amy has. Says she's moving again."

"Where to?"

"Michigan."

"Damn." Dominic shook his head, kicking the ground with his boot and squinting at the glare of the setting sun. "You talk her out of it yet?"

"No." Logan cut his eyes to Dominic. "And don't go bringing it up. Betty doesn't know yet, and Amy only told Traci she was moving to a new apartment, not where. Amy hasn't had time to settle in. She gets to feeling cornered, she'll pack up and leave. Then I won't have a chance in hell of getting her to stay."

"Well, if you ever do need me to talk to her, just say the word."

Logan scoffed. "She's *my* wife. If anyone talks to her, it'll be me."

Dominic stilled, a slow smile spreading across his face. "Well, hell, bro. You're getting hard-core in your old age, yeah?"

A burst of laughter broke from Logan's chest and the tension faded from his limbs. He loved having his brother back home again. He grabbed the back of Dominic's neck and squeezed, giving him a playful shake.

"Old? If you know what's good for you, you'll cut that shit out."

Dominic laughed and shoved him off. "I'll believe that when I see it."

Logan smiled and led the way over to the paddock to join Amy. She leaned further over the top rail of the fence as several horses milled around the enclosure. She pointed at a golden stallion standing a head taller than the rest, his white mane rippling with each movement of his broad neck.

"Is that my Lightning?" she asked.

"Yeah." A wave of pleasure swept through Logan at the eager expression on her face. "You're welcome to tuck him in for the night." He lowered his voice to a teasing tone. "That is, if you can make it over the fence and across the field in that stuffy getup."

Dominic chuckled at his side and Amy smirked, a hint of her old spirit shining in her eyes.

"That won't be necessary," she said.

She inhaled and whistled around two fingers. The melodic sound traveled across the expanse of the paddock, perking up the horses' ears and rebounding off the stable walls. Lightning shot to attention, spun and galloped toward the fence. He drew to a halt, dipping his broad head over the top rail and nuzzling his nose against her shoulder.

"Good boy," she crooned, kissing Lightning's forehead and resting her dark head against his thick neck. "You're still a beauty."

"He oughta be a beauty," Dominic said. "Logan's been babying him for the last four years."

Logan grunted, rubbing Lightning's back. "There's nothing wrong with a little extra attention. And he deserved it. He's pulled his weight on the trails. Every new guest we get requests him." He looked up to find Amy's eyes clinging to his. "You trained him well."

Amy rolled her lips, a smile fighting at the corners of her mouth. "I wasn't alone in that. Besides, you were the one that trained me, remember?"

"I remember," he whispered.

He reached out and tucked a loose strand of her hair behind her ear. The silky feel of it lingered on his fingertips, heating his blood.

Amy stepped back, eyes sifting through the rest of the horses. "Where's Thunder?"

Logan stiffened. Of course she'd ask about Thunder. That black stallion had always been one of her favorites, along with Lightning. He curled his fists around the fence rail.

"Logan?" Amy's hands covered his, her face creased with worry. "Where is he?"

Logan glanced at Dominic. He winced, his dark eyes moving to hover over the stables in the distance.

Logan sighed. He should've prepared for this. Should've had something ready to say. The last thing Amy needed right now was bad news and he didn't want to be the one to deliver it. Unfortunately, there was no way around this.

Logan shoved off the fence and took Amy's hand in his, rubbing his thumb over the fragile skin of her wrist. "Come on. I'll take you to him."

AMY SHIVERED. THE warmth of the sun faded and the approaching darkness sent a chill through the air. It sliced beneath her flesh and traveled to her bones, forcing her to huddle closer to Logan's side. His big hand tugged, leading her away from the paddock and down the winding trail to the stables.

The tight set of Logan's jaw and his continued silence froze the blood in her veins. She scanned the path before them, following the familiar curves to the stable where she'd spent the majority of her childhood days.

Every morning, she'd raced to the stalls to plop at Logan's feet and watch him groom the horses. And every afternoon, she'd returned to lean in the doorway and wait for his return. The image of him mounted on his horse, slowly crossing the field, seemed emblazoned on her memory. She was certain the image of her idolizing expression remained imprinted on his.

Her face flamed despite the cool bite of winter air. Amy lifted her chin and straightened the collar of her blouse with her free hand. None of it mattered. There wasn't any point in seeking out old comforts. Or reliving past humiliations. She wasn't staying long enough to enjoy one or endure the other.

She craned her neck, peering past the open doors of the stable for a glimpse of Thunder's dark hair. She knew the exact shade. Years ago, when she'd delivered the foal, she'd stayed to watch Thunder rise on trembling legs then spent the next week smoothing her hands over his black mane.

Logan's hand tightened around hers and he slowed his step. "There was an accident a couple of months ago." He stopped inside the stable entrance, drawing her to a halt. "One of the guests took Thunder out without permission. Some arrogant young suit on vacation, playing at being a rancher for the week."

His mouth firmed into a tight line, throat moving on a hard swallow.

"He knew Thunder was a jumper. Drove him over a few fences and off the lot." He released her, hands shoving deep into his pockets. "Raintree probably looked endless to him, being a city boy and all. He left the ranch and ran Thunder right into the highway." He looked back across the empty fields, shoulders sagging. "Those transfer trucks don't stop for anything out here. Don't know if he was trying to race or didn't see the truck coming, but their paths crossed."

Amy froze. Thunder was a strong stallion, ripped

with muscled bulk and impressive speed. But he'd be no match for a transfer truck. Not the kind that sped along the isolated highways surrounding Raintree.

"Was he...?" Her throat constricted, the question catching.

"No." Logan's black eyes shot to her face and his deep voice softened. "You know Thunder. He's not going down without a fight." A grim smile curved his lips. "He reared, bucked that boy off him and jumped. Almost made it out of the way." His expression darkened. "But almosts don't cut it. He got clipped and was banged up pretty bad. We thought for sure he wouldn't last the night but he did. He's not the same, though. Whole thing scarred him bad. Turned him wild. None of us have been able to make any headway with him."

Amy scanned the empty stalls lining the stable, eyes scrambling from one to the next.

"Only thing that saved the guest was Thunder's instincts," Logan said. "That kid came out of it with a few cuts and bruises. A lot less than he deserved." He cleared his throat. "I wish I'd kept a closer eye on him. He was a reckless rider. And a selfish one to boot."

Amy took in the hard set of Logan's jaw. He'd always been controlled and practical but he had a soft spot for his horses. Often went to extremes to protect and care for them. It was one of the many things she still admired about him.

She touched his arm, fingers resting lightly against the hard curve of his bicep. "You're not meant to control people any more than horses. You can only lead them. How many times did you tell me that over the years?"

Amy's gut clenched, a surge of shameful heat flooding her. Logan had repeated the mantra a thousand times when she'd struggled with training a horse. She could still see his somber expression as he'd delivered the sentiment, but she'd never really listened. Instead, she'd pushed the boundaries of their friendship and tempted him into a different relationship. Had tried to control him all the same.

Logan withdrew his hand from his pocket, capturing hers and smoothing his thumb over her wrist. "He's not the same, Amy. You still want to see him?"

She nodded.

Logan took her elbow, guiding her down the aisle past the empty stalls to a large one tucked in the back. An eerie stillness settled around them. The front of the stall remained empty, a dark bulk huddling in the back corner.

Heart pounding, Amy leaned closer and secured her purse strap on her shoulder with shaky fingers.

"Hey, boy," she whispered.

There was no response. Only the stallion's heavy breathing disturbed the silence.

"Thunder?" She took a small step forward, palm pressing to the stall guard and fingers wrapping around the bars. "Hey, b—"

A hoof slammed into the bars, the edge of it ramming against her knuckles and rattling the stall door on its frame. Amy jumped back, heels clacking over the bricked floor and catching on the slight crevices in between. One cracked loose in the process.

Logan's strong arms wrapped around her right before she slammed into the floor. Her purse dropped from her shoulder and tangled around her ankles, contents spilling out. The relentless pounding continued, Thunder's kicks increasing in intensity and echoing around them.

"Are you okay?" Logan reached for her injured hand.

"I'm fine," she choked.

She drew her throbbing fingers to her chest, cradling them and gritting her teeth.

"Let me see." Logan's brow creased and he tugged at her wrist.

"It's fine," she bit out, stifling a grimace. "He skimmed me."

The kicking stopped. Amy glanced up as the strong pull and push of Thunder's heaving breaths grew close. His broad head appeared against the bars. A savage scar stretched across his chiseled face and down his muscular neck. Amy winced at his glare, the whites of his eyes stark against the wide and wild depths of his pupils.

"He's been through a lot," Logan said. "It's changed him. In the beginning, I thought there was still a chance I could bring him around. But I lost his trust along the way. I'm out of options. I have to put him down."

"No," she whispered.

Thunder's lips drew back and he cried, the sharp sound screeching through the air and splitting her ears. He slammed his front hooves against the door then jerked away to pace the stall, his pained cries turning fierce.

Amy's legs shook. She bent carefully to gather up the contents of her purse. Shoving the scattered items back inside, she caught sight of the bundle of crumpled divorce papers. She snatched them up and drove them deep into her purse.

Metal clanked as Thunder dove forward and butted the stall door with his head. Eyes flaring, he fixed his gaze to hers and stared deep, tearing past the layers of her polished appearance and creeping beneath her skin. He jerked his head, screaming louder and kicking harder.

Amy choked back a sob and shoved to her feet. Logan was right. Thunder wasn't the same. But to consider ending his life...

"You can't put him down, Logan," she said, turning away and stumbling on the loose heel of her shoe. "Not without giving him a fair shot."

Logan held her arms and steadied her. "I have. Nothing has worked. He's a danger to himself and the other horses and he's especially aggressive around the boys. There's not one single rehabilitation outfit willing to relocate him after laying eyes on him." He sighed. "I can't, in good conscience, allow him to exist in fear and isolation with no quality of life. I'm sorry. There's nothing else that can be done."

Amy ducked her burning face. "That's not true," she said, pushing past him. "There's always a way."

The urge to return to Thunder was strong. To stay at his side, try to coax his spirit back and give him a fighting chance. But that would mean staying. And it was time to move on.

She dragged her purse strap back onto her shoulder and brushed at her clothes. But even though the creases in the material released, the guilt remained. It clung to her skin and clogged her throat, suffocating her. Just as it had every day for the past four years.

Her steps slowed, legs stilling of their own accord. She cast one last look at Thunder's violent attack on the stall. "Surely, there's something you can d—"

Thunder's screech overtook her voice, the words dying on her lips.

"He fought hard to survive, Amy." Logan's expression turned grim, his thumb spinning the ring on his finger. "But, sometimes, that's just not enough."

She spun, taking swift strides out of the stable and away from the stallion's broken state. She'd worked hard to survive, too. And she couldn't gamble the new life she'd fought for to recapture a past full of failures and sins.

Logan's eyes bored into her back. Amy hurried up the hill, thighs burning. Thunder's painful cries lingered on the air, hovering around her and haunting the path to the main house.

Chapter Three

"Hold on to your heart, girl."

Amy whispered the words and pressed her fingertips to the cold metal of Logan's truck. By the time she'd made her way back from the stables, the sun had disappeared and night had settled in. The full moon and stars cast a hazy glow over the surrounding fields, lengthening the shadows stretching from the fences and barn.

She grazed her throbbing knuckles over the ring hidden beneath her collar and grimaced, recalling the band on Logan's hand. Her chest tightened. She shook her head, reached into the bed of Logan's truck and hefted out one of her black bags.

"Here." Logan's chest brushed her back. He reached around her for the bag, his fingers brushing hers. "Let me."

"I've got it."

Amy hoisted the bag and leaned over to retrieve the second one. Logan scooped it up first. He flicked the cuff of his flannel shirt back and examined the glowing hands of his wristwatch.

"It's almost six," he said. "We better get a move on."

He led the way up the drive toward the main house, the strong line of his back and lean jean-clad hips moving with confidence. Amy's belly fluttered. She tore her eyes away and surveyed the entrance to the main house which was bathed in the soft glow of the porch lights.

Massive mahogany doors were adorned with lush green wreaths and red ribbons. The colorful cheer extended beyond the wreaths to the crimson ribbon wrapped around the large columns. Poinsettia blooms nestled in the nooks and crannies of the railing lining the porch and the warm glow emanating from inside the house enhanced the twinkling of the white lights draping the posts and eaves.

Christmas. Amy's steps faltered on the slippery ground. It'd been so long since she'd spent the holidays at home with family. Since she'd left Raintree, the color and comfort of Christmas had faded and the holiday had contorted into a pale passing of a day. A low and lifeless one she'd grown accustomed to spending alone.

Amy swallowed the lump in her throat and strived for a light tone. "Why are all the decorations out already? Mama used to say it was a sin to put up Christmas lights before Thanksgiving was over."

Logan glanced over his shoulder, his words reaching her in puffy, white drifts. "I imagine Betty was beside herself last night when we didn't make it back like we'd planned. She probably got overanxious and decided to keep herself busy."

Amy smiled. Next to cooking, her mother's second favorite pastime was decorating. Not a single holiday passed without Betty celebrating it in style.

"Betty knows how much you used to love Christmas at Raintree." Logan waited for her to reach his side, his big palm wrapping around her upper arm to assist her up the steps. "She wants to make this visit perfect for you. We all do."

Amy's blood rushed at the husky note in his voice and she curled her fingers around the handle of her bag, tamping down the urge to lean in to him.

Hold on to your heart. This time, she wouldn't mistake friendship for love. What she felt for Logan was old-fashioned lust and misguided hero worship. She'd do well to remember that.

A loud jingle sounded, both wreaths swinging on their doors as a small figure burst out of the house.

"Amy."

Betty's red bangs ruffled in the night breeze, her green eyes glistening with moisture.

Amy's vision blurred. "Hi, Mama."

She drew her bag in against her thigh and dipped toward the floor of the porch, the length of her limbs becoming awkward. Betty's short stature had always made Amy wither, trying not to loom over her.

Betty's warm palms cradled her cool cheeks then traveled down her arms to caress her wrists. She gently lifted Amy's arms out to the side, trailing her gaze from the top of her head to the tips of her shoes.

"You look beautiful. I think you grew another inch since I saw you last. You're just as tall as your father was." Betty dabbed at the corners of her eyes and smiled. "I'm so glad you came home." She stretched up on her tiptoes, her kiss grazing the curve of Amy's jaw. "I've missed my sweet girl."

"I've missed you, too."

Much more than she'd realized. Amy wrapped her arms around her mother in a tight embrace. The rich scent of cinnamon and butter lingered on Betty's white chef's apron, releasing in sweet puffs with each of Amy's squeezes.

Amy giggled and nuzzled her cheek against Betty's silken hair. "You smell like cookies."

"That's because I've been baking your favorite ones all afternoon."

"Cinnamon and sugar?"

"Stacked a mile high," Betty said, laughing. She released Amy and tugged at Logan's shoulders, kissing his cheek when he bent his head. "Thank you for bringing her home safely, Logan. I was worried the storm would keep you from making it."

"You think we'd let a bit of ice keep us from your cooking?" A crooked grin broke out across Logan's face and his dark eyes sparkled. "Not a chance."

Betty patted his broad chest, her smile widening. "I made your favorites, too. The green bean casserole and sweet potato soufflé are ready and waiting." She shivered and rubbed her arms. "Let's get inside. It's too chilly out here for comfort."

Logan nudged the small of Amy's back, spurring her step on. She followed Betty's jubilant advance into the cheery interior of the house and found the spacious foyer as warm and welcoming as it'd been in the past. The rich grain of the hardwood floors gleamed, several coats hung from a hall tree bench by the entrance and festive garlands draped elegantly from each banister of the winding staircase.

The low rumble of voices, children laughing and silverware clinking sounded from a large room on the right. Two teenage girls dressed in green-and-black chef uniforms strolled by carting pitchers of iced tea and water.

"You've hired some help, I see," Amy said, noting the girls' bright smiles and energetic expressions.

Betty nodded. "Raintree has done well the last two years. We've had to renovate the family floor and expand to accommodate more guests." Her eyes brightened. "Logan and Cissy started an apprenticeship program for high school students last year. We have positions for students interested in culinary arts and equine management and the school gives them class credit on a work-based learning program. The kids learn and make money at the same time. And, believe me, those teenagers are a Godsend in the kitchen around the holidays." She smirked. "Wish I could get your sister to peel potatoes as willingly as they do."

Amy laughed. "I'd pay good money to see that."

She glanced at Logan, warming at his lopsided grin. It was reminiscent of him as a teenager. Even then, he'd taken an eager interest in the business side of Raintree and had been determined to build it into a successful guest ranch. From the looks of things, he'd succeeded.

"Seems you're doing a great job managing Raintree," she said. "You must be proud."

Logan shrugged. "It was mostly Cissy's doing. She and the twins didn't have much when Dom brought them to Raintree, and she knows how some families struggle. She wanted local kids to have as many opportunities as possible to succeed." His smile widened. "Dom's even getting in on the action. He's trying to talk a friend into partnering so he can offer bull riding clinics."

Amy smiled. "That's wonderful."

The warmth in Logan's smile traveled upward to pool in his black eyes. The pleased gleam in them calmed her pulse and parted her lips. Lord, how she'd missed him. Missed talking to him, sharing dreams and celebrating successes. She missed her best friend.

"There's our girl," a deep voice rumbled.

Amy spun, a giggle escaping her as a tall, gray-haired man approached. Tate Slade, Logan's father, had always held a special place in her heart. Having lost her dad to a heart attack at age seven, Amy had found a second father in Tate—or Pop, as everyone called him—as soon as they arrived at Raintree. His familiar gait and handsome smile provoked a fresh surge of tears. Pop pulled her close for a gentle hug and she pressed her cheek to his broad chest.

"It's so good to have you home for a while," Pop murmured.

"I'm glad to be back."

He kissed her forehead, stepped back and nodded at Logan. "You made it back right on time. The guests have already settled in for Thanksgiving dinner and Betty has almost finished setting up the family table."

Logan slipped the bag from Amy's shoulder. "I'll get Amy set up in a room and we'll be there in a minute.

"Don't think that's possible." Pop hesitated, splaying his hands. "A lot of guests missed their flights yesterday because of the storm. We've had to extend their stays and ended up with double bookings. Everything's packed tight. Except for y'all's—" he winced, nodding at Logan "—I mean, your room."

Logan flushed. His knuckles tightened around the handles of the bags and he shifted from foot to foot. Betty fidgeted with the hem of her apron and Pop studied the toes of his boots. The silence lengthened and Amy's heart ached at the awkward discomfort.

Logan cleared his throat. "I'll stay in one of the bunkhouses. You can have my room."

"Thank you, Logan." Amy rubbed her clammy palms over her pants legs and forced a smile. "Mama, how about I help you finish setting the table while Logan puts my bags up?"

Betty's face creased with relief. "Perfect. I'll go get Cissy. It's high time the two of you met."

"And I'll round up the boys." Pop winked as he left. "Lord knows where they are."

Amy started toward the kitchen, faltering when Logan gripped her arm.

"You've got to tell her about the move…"

"I will." Amy sighed, a sharp pain settling behind her eyes. "But I'm not going to spring it on her this second." She rubbed her brow with her fingertips. "I'll tell her later. At a better time. Let's just have a pleasant dinner for now, okay?"

She pulled away and headed down the hall. Her gut churned at the thought of telling her mother and sister about moving so far away. The last thing she wanted to do was upset anyone during her first visit home in ages. But, eventually, there'd be no way around it.

The light aroma of cinnamon enveloped Amy as she entered Raintree's large kitchen. She inhaled, pulling in a lungful of the familiar scent. A red platter piled high with cookies sat on the edge of the kitchen island and her mouth watered.

Out of habit, Amy snuck a look over her shoulder at the empty doorway, half expecting Betty to spring into the room and shoo her away. As kids, she and Traci had never been successful at snagging a cookie before dinner without Betty pointing a finger and ushering them out. She smiled and made her way over to the cookies.

She reached out and stopped, hand hovering in mid-air. Small, grubby fingers fumbled over the pile of sugar cookies. Mud-streaked fingertips curled around the edge of one and tugged it toward the edge of the plate.

Amy leaned over and found the top of a blond head pressed below the edge of the counter. The head swiveled and deep blue eyes widened up at her in shock. She bit back her grin and narrowed her eyes, taking in his features. Could be Kayden. But the twins were so similar in appearance it was hard to be sure.

"Shhh," the boy whispered. "Don't tell."

"Boys." A short woman with blond hair peeked around the door and leveled a stern expression across the room. "Stop that and get over here."

The boy jumped, his head banging into the edge of the counter. He jerked his hand from the cookies and several scattered to the floor. Another blond head shot up from the other side of the island. This one was definitely Kayden. He sported the same cavalier expression he'd displayed earlier when Logan had chastised him. The boys stood together, Jayden with a bowed head and Kayden with raised brows.

"What'd we do, Aunt Cissy?" Kayden asked, a dab of red cinnamon icing smudged across his cheek.

"You know very well what you did," she said. "Now, get those cookies up and go wash your hands. You're about to eat supper."

The boys groaned but complied, gathering up the broken cookies and tossing them in the trash.

The woman winced and shot Amy a rueful smile. "Sorry about that. Those two are always looking for trouble. You must be Amy. I'm so glad to finally meet you. I'm Cissy, Dom's wife."

Cissy entered the kitchen, stepping carefully and pressing a palm to the blue sweater stretched across her heavily pregnant belly. Amy froze. Her eyes clung to the roundness of Cissy's midsection and her arms drew in against the flat emptiness of her own. Weight dragged at her legs, rooting her to the floor.

Amy swallowed hard and held out a shaky hand. Cissy covered it with both of hers. She was a tiny thing, her shoulders barely reaching Amy's chest. But her blue eyes were rich with welcome and happiness.

"I've heard so many wonderful things about you," Cissy said.

Amy masked her expression with a polite smile. That couldn't be the case. There weren't that many good things for anyone to tell.

"Dominic talks so much about how you two got up to no good back in the day," Cissy added with a laugh.

That sounded more like it.

"So this is where you boys snuck off to." Betty swept in, smiling as the twins rushed over and wrapped their arms around her waist.

"We're hungry," Jayden said, tipping his head back and pouting.

"Yeah." Kayden frowned. "And Aunt Cissy won't let us have a cookie."

"I'll let you have one," Cissy said. "*After* supper. I'm sorry, Betty." She flashed an apologetic smile. "The boys were supposed to be washing up with Traci. Not sneaking away and stealing cookies."

"Aw, come on, Aunt Cissy," Kayden said. "You can

smell 'em all the way down the hall. And we only wanted one."

"You can have one after you eat dinner. Not before."

Kayden poked a grubby finger at Amy. "But she's gonna eat one."

Betty ruffled their shiny hair and laughed. "Well, she should know better. I never let her or Traci get away with grabbing a cookie before dinner either."

Jayden elbowed his brother. "Hush, Kayden. Aunt Amy didn't rat *us* out, you know." He nodded up at Betty. "Aunt Amy can have one. We'll wait 'til later." He jerked his chin at his brother. "Come on."

The two boys scampered out, pausing to press a quick kiss to Cissy's belly.

"Can't blame them for trying." Cissy giggled and rubbed her palm in smooth circles over her protruding midsection. "Even the girls kick harder when I get close enough to smell your mother's cookies."

Girls. Amy stared at Cissy's middle. She'd almost had a girl of her own. *Sara.*

The ache behind Amy's eyes spread, streaking in painful bolts to her temples. Heaven help her, she thought she'd gotten past this. Thought she'd set this pain down long ago.

"Congratulations," Amy managed to choke out on a strangled whisper.

"Thanks." Cissy laughed. "We're having twins. Once you add the boys, Dom and I are in for quadruple the trouble. But I wouldn't have it any other way."

Betty's arm curled around Amy's waist and squeezed. Lines of worry creased her brow.

Amy lifted her chin, hugged Betty closer to her side

and summoned up a sincere smile. "I'm so happy for you both. Dom's a good man."

Cissy nodded. "One of the best."

Betty lifted to her toes and kissed Amy's cheek. "Well, I think it's about time we got a home-cooked meal in you. Whatcha say we get this table set?"

Ten minutes later and only five minutes beyond Betty's designated six-o'clock dinner hour, the family Thanksgiving table was packed. Utensils clanged, napkins flapped in the air and settled in laps. Dishes stuffed with sweet and savory samplings were passed from one end of the table to the other.

The twins, tucked snugly between Cissy and Dominic, barely paused to breathe between bites. Traci ate with the same enthusiasm, shooting smiles Amy's way between each extra helping. Logan went for seconds, his muscular arm brushing against her as he stretched across the table.

Amy shifted in her seat, still whirling from the rush of reunions and welcomes. The only moment she'd had to herself was when the men had left to check on the guests while Betty and Cissy rounded up the boys and Traci. Amy had seized the opportunity to sneak off and stow her purse in her bedroom.

She winced. *Their* bedroom. Hers and Logan's. The same room they'd first shared on the night of their wedding, dodging each other's eyes with tight smiles and stiff limbs as they'd prepared for bed. Her guilt and his anger at her betrayal had made it difficult to enjoy the occasion.

Amy's leg quivered at the brush of Logan's thigh under the table. She slid to the side, lifting her cold glass of sweet tea and taking a deep swallow. The liquid coated her throat and forced its way past the lump lodged there. A chill swept through her, raising goose bumps on her arms.

There was no way she'd be able to sleep in that bed. Not with all the memories filling that room. And not with Logan's familiar scent of soap and pine lingering on the sheets.

She put the glass down with trembling fingers and picked a loose strand of hair off her neck, tucking it back into the topknot that had almost fallen loose.

"Here, baby girl."

Pop stretched across the table and tipped the large pitcher of tea toward her glass.

"No, thanks, Pop. I've got plenty."

"Saving room for the sweet stuff at the end, huh?" he asked, setting the pitcher down.

Amy nodded, trying for a small smile.

"She gwanna eat le cookies wif us." Kayden's mouth gaped around a lump of potatoes.

"Ew." Traci wrinkled her nose. "Swallow your food first, squirt."

Dominic chuckled, wiping Kayden's mouth with a napkin. "Use your manners, buddy."

Jayden snickered at his brother.

"You, too, Jayden," Cissy said, plucking a bit of turkey from his lap and putting it on the edge of his plate.

They all laughed and some of Amy's tension eased. She took a bite of green bean casserole.

"Nothing quite like a full house." Pop sat back in his chair and sighed with satisfaction. "Sure is nice having all of you kids back home at the same time."

Betty murmured an assent, casting a wistful look at Amy. "It's wonderful. I'm so grateful to have you back for a few weeks. I just wish it was longer. Will you be able to visit again this summer?"

The painful throb returned behind Amy's eyes. She'd have a new job by then. There was no chance of her being able to take time off work again that soon after moving to Michigan and hope to make a good impression. She shrugged with stiff shoulders.

"I don't think so, Mama. I'd hate to take up a room during the busy season. You told me yourself Raintree is always full now. Especially around the holidays." Amy gestured toward the closed door leading to the public dining room. "There's a crowd out there."

"Yeah, but those are guests." Pop smiled, eyes warming. "You're family. We always have room for family."

Betty squeezed Amy's arm. "And your seat's been empty for far too long." She smiled at Logan. "We're all so happy you've come home."

"That we are," Logan added in a low voice, his warm palm smoothing over her back.

Amy's face heated. She straightened, the cup tilting in her hand and ice clinking in the empty glass.

"Switch gears," Dominic said, propping the mouth of a wine bottle on the edge of her glass and sloshing red liquid into it.

"No, thanks. I'm good." Amy nudged the bottle away.

The red stream splashed against the ivory tablecloth. The formal one with the fancy cutwork and scalloped lace edges. Betty's favorite.

Amy gasped and dabbed at the rapidly spreading stain with her napkin. "Oh, I'm so sorry, Mama."

Betty tsked, shaking her head and stilling Amy's hand. "Don't trouble yourself. We've got more where that came from."

"You sure you don't want a glass of wine?" Dominic asked, concern clouding his features. "You had a long trip down here. It'll help you relax a bit."

Amy pressed harder at the soaked tablecloth with her napkin. "No, I'm fine. A bit tired is all."

Dominic exchanged a glance with Logan before averting his face and returning to his meal.

"She needs a good night's rest," Logan murmured. "We had a long day and a run-in with Thunder earlier." He took the napkin from her hand, leaning close and gently examining her swollen knuckles. "How're they feeling?"

Amy's skin tingled under his tender touch. She shrugged, peeled her eyes from his dark five-o'clock shadow and chiseled jaw and ignored his enticing male scent.

"We're sorry about Thunder," Pop said. "Real sorry, Amy. We all know how much you love that horse. Wish we didn't have to put him down."

Amy's throat closed and she couldn't bring herself to meet Pop's eyes.

"Whatcha mean, put him down?" Jayden's brow creased.

"Yeah," Kayden said. "What's gonna happen to him, Aunt Cissy?"

Cissy moved to speak but stopped, shaking her head and looking down at the table.

"He doesn't have to be put down," Traci said, blinking back tears. "You could help him, Amy."

Logan leveled a look across the table. "Traci, Thunder is beyond anyone's help. And now's not the time to discu—"

"When *would* be the time?" Traci asked, shooting

a pleading look at Betty. "Tell her, Mama. You know she's the only one that could do it."

Betty sighed but asked gently, "Have you given any thought to working with him, Amy?"

"That would take a lot of time," Amy said. "More time than I have."

"But they're gonna put him down." Traci's voice rose. "Please, Amy. I'll help you. I've been training the other horses and Logan said I have a way with them. Just like you. Isn't that right, Logan?"

Logan nodded slowly, his steady gaze causing Amy's cheeks to tingle. "She's not where you were at her age but she's good." His smile was tender. "It must be in your blood."

"See?" Traci scooted forward in her chair and rested her fists on the edge of the table. "Come on, Amy. It won't take us that long. And if it does, surely you can stay for a few extra days."

Amy fixed her eyes on the red stain bleeding toward the edge of the table. "I can't."

Traci glowered. "Why not?"

"Traci," Betty admonished.

"Not 'til she tells me why."

"That's enough, Traci." Logan's arm tensed against Amy. "It's too dangerous. And she just said—"

"I know what she said but she can't mean it." Traci's voice shook. "They're gonna *put him down*, Amy. Don't you care about Thunder at all?"

"I care. But I can't stay."

Amy closed her eyes briefly, her good intentions fading. Now was as good a time as any to tell them. This might be the best opportunity she'd get to break the news.

"I can't stay any longer than I'd planned because I've been offered a management position. It's one I've worked really hard for and I start in January."

Betty smiled. "That's wonderful news. Is it with the same insurance company?"

"Yes, but it's at a new branch." She licked her lips. "In Michigan."

Her quiet comment pierced the comfortable companionship at the table and thickened the air around them. The clatter of utensils silenced.

"Michigan?" Betty's chin quivered and her eyes glistened. "But that's so far away."

"It's not that bad a trip by plane, Mama," she said gently. "You and Traci can visit as much as you want. I'll buy the tickets."

Amy glanced at Traci. Her eyes flooded and tears streamed from her lashes down her cheeks.

"You told me you were moving to a new apartment. Not to a different state." Traci's ragged whisper broke the silence at the table.

She rose, pushing back her chair and leaving the room.

"Come on, boys," Cissy said, pulling the twins' napkins from their laps and nudging them to their feet. "Time for your bath."

Kayden scowled. "But we ain't had no cookies yet. You said we could—"

"I'll get you some on the way," Dominic said. He stood, helped Cissy up with a hand on her elbow then took each of the boys' hands, leading them out of the room.

"Have you thought this through?" Betty asked, fingers clutching the collar of her shirt. "Maybe you need to take some time and decide if it's really what you want to do."

"I'm sure, Mama."

"But…" Betty's gaze hovered on a red-faced Logan. "What about…?"

"Things have been over for a long time between me and Logan," Amy whispered. "You know that. It was my fault. I was too young and too much happe—" Her voice broke and she cleared her throat. "It's time we both moved on."

The implication fell hard, slamming into the silence and echoing around the room. Betty winced and looked at Pop. A burst of laughter traveled from the guests' dining room, the sound muffled by the closed door.

"Logan?" Pop frowned, his gaze sharp on his son's face.

Logan's jaw clenched. He looked down and slumped back in his chair.

"Excuse me," Betty whispered, shaking her head and leaving the table.

The sound of her sobs faded with each of her slow steps.

"I'll just…give you two a minute." Pop squeezed Logan's shoulder briefly before he left, too.

Amy stayed silent, flinching at the harsh rasp of Logan's heavy breaths and staring at the empty chairs. She bit her lip, her teeth digging hard into the soft flesh, and a sharp metallic flavor trickled onto her tongue. Red drops of wine dripped from the tablecloth and plopped onto her leg, the crisp material of her pinstriped pants soggy beneath the stain.

The moment was so familiar. Almost a perfect replica of another meal she'd shared at this table. When she'd announced her pregnancy with gleeful, nineteen-year-old abandon, shocking and saddening those around her. Betty's tears and Pop's disapproval had been just as strong. And Logan's shame just as apparent.

Amy jerked to her feet and headed for the door with unsteady steps. She shouldn't have told them tonight. It hadn't been the right time. But she'd done so anyway because it was easiest for her.

Here, she was still the same disruptive girl she'd always been. If she stayed at Raintree, she'd only bring more of the same. Discord and trouble. She should never have come back.

Chapter Four

It'd be so easy to let her go. To turn around, trudge to their room—which had been empty of her for so long—and continue with the status quo.

Logan frowned, examining the stiff line of Amy's back through the window. He clutched the bottle of beer in his hand, the cold wetness seeping into his warm skin. It was Amy's favorite brand. The only kind she drank. And he'd kept it on hand for four years, fool that he was, having picked it up out of habit during every trip to town.

He'd grabbed the bottle quickly from the fridge minutes earlier, ducking out of the kitchen to the low murmurs of Pop consoling a tearful Betty, then made his way toward the front porch. To do the right thing. To talk to Amy and pick up the pieces. Again.

He rolled his shoulders, trying to ease the knot in his upper back. His mind urged him to walk away. It practically screamed at him to go in the opposite direction. Just as it had yesterday morning when he'd sat in his truck debating whether or not to make the trip to bring her home.

But, just like then, something inside propelled him toward her. It burned hot in his chest, searing his hands and making him desperate to hold on. Even though he knew it was a high risk. Amy's passionate nature had never been predictable and it was even less trustworthy.

He gritted his teeth. Hell if he'd be like Pop and stand in Raintree's dirt drive watching his wife drive away. Crumple into a weak heap as she left her family behind. He was stronger than that.

Logan looked away, peering past the Christmas lights strung along the porch rail to the dark night beyond. Pop had been little good to himself back when his wife left. Much less to his sons. Ten at the time, Logan hadn't sat idly by. Instead, he'd picked up the reins of the ranch, hustled through the daily chores and watched out for his wild younger brother, refusing to allow himself to dwell on his mother's absence or his father's grief.

His mother had made the decision to leave and Logan had accepted it. It was her loss, not theirs. He just wished his father had seen things the same way. The way Logan should accept Amy's decision to leave now.

He dropped his gaze, tracing the trails of condensation on the glass bottle. Amy's movements brought his eyes back to her. She shifted from one ridiculous high heel to the other, leaning down to prop her elbows on the porch rail and wrap her arms around herself with a shiver.

Logan sighed. It was barely above thirty degrees outside and there his stubborn wife stood. Freezing her tail off.

His heart tripped in his chest. *His wife. His Amy.*

He should leave things alone. Let her go her way and him his, as Traci had urged in the office lobby of limbo. But despite it all, he needed her back. Needed *them* back. The way they were before she'd shot their relationship to all hell and beyond.

Amy owed it to him. And they both owed it to their daughter's memory. Otherwise, their baby girl would be nothing more than a mistake. An almost that never drew breath. A wrong that was never righted.

He closed his eyes and hung his head, muscles flinching on a jagged streak of anger. At himself. At Amy. God forgive him for feeling it but it was there all the same.

Logan made his way outside, boots scraping across the floor and drawing to a halt behind Amy. He set the unopened beer on the porch rail and drew in a lungful of icy air.

"Here." He shrugged off his denim jacket, draping it over her bent form.

Amy wanted to refuse it. The urge to decline was written in her drawn brows and scrunched nose. But she accepted it.

"Thanks." She hunched into the coat and turned back to the dark emptiness before them.

Despite his ill mood, a smile tugged at his lips. Amy had always been stubborn. Head thick as a brick but sharp as a tack, she'd fought him at every turn. It'd started the day they'd met. At eight years old, she'd given him a run for his money. She'd sized up his twelve-year-old frame, curled her lip and dared him to race her. And damned if she hadn't won.

Logan eased his hip against the rail and crossed his arms, a low laugh escaping him.

"You still know how to make an entrance." He nudged her and eyed the tight line of her mouth. "Family dinners always were a lot more interesting with you around."

Her shoulders stiffened and she leaned down, propping her elbows on the porch rail and twisting her hands together.

"You plan on spending the night out here?" he asked.

"Maybe."

"Doubt you'd last long, cold as it is."

She glanced up then, emerald eyes fixing firmly on his face. "I'd last long enough."

Logan grunted. He scooped up the beer bottle, snagged the cap on the porch rail and snapped it off. He tipped the bottle up and tugged deeply, swallowing several mouthfuls of the smooth brew and sighing with pleasure.

Amy's gaze clung to him, following the movements of his throat and darting to his hand. He took another swig. Her eyebrows lowered into a glower.

Logan's belly warmed, sending a sweet thrill up his spine. She'd had the exact same expression the night of her nineteenth birthday. He'd given in to her badgering and had taken her up to the local pool hall to celebrate.

She hadn't been satisfied with flashing her ID at the door. Nope. She'd done her best to sweet talk him into going to the bar and getting her a beer. He'd brought her fried cheese sticks and a milk instead. She'd been beyond ticked.

The warmth spread to his face and pulled at the corners of his mouth. He tipped the bottle up again, grinning as her frown darkened. It was good to see a little life in her.

She jerked her chin. "Your daddy ever tell you it's impolite not to share?"

A chuckle rumbled deep in his chest. The kind he hadn't had in years. He let it loose, relishing the feel and sound of it.

Her gaze wandered over his face to linger on his smile. Her lush mouth parted, the edges tipping up and her face lighting with pleasure. That was all it took.

Before he knew it, he was leaning over, savoring the curves of her lips under his. The sweet flavor of her mingled with the crisp coolness of the beer on his tongue.

She tasted the same. Warm and comforting. Like his own personal sun in the middle of winter. She tasted like home.

It didn't last. She pulled away, squaring her shoulders and stepping back.

"This can't happen, Logan," she whispered.

"Why not?" He straightened, setting the beer back on the porch rail. "You're still my wife."

"I haven't been that for a long time. And I wouldn't have been in the first place if you'd had a choice."

"That's not true—"

"It's not?" She leaned forward. "You mean if I hadn't lied to you and gotten pregnant, you would've chosen to marry me?"

He hesitated, scrambling for the right words. The ones he'd chosen so carefully on the drive to bring her home.

"You've never lied to me, Logan. Please don't start now," she stated softly. "Would you have married me back then if you'd had a choice?"

Not then. Not at such a young age. And not before they'd had a chance to experience life beyond the ranch.

His jaw clamped shut. He couldn't say that out loud. Not now. Not when she looked so vulnerable. So hopeful.

"Would you have given in to me to begin with if I hadn't trailed you so hard? If I hadn't pushed so much?" she pressed, her voice catching.

No. He wouldn't have.

She sighed and looked away. "We grew up together. We were friends. I should've left it at that."

That cool mask returned. It settled over her features like a glaze of ice, freezing out all emotion in her expression.

"You were right," she said, knuckles turning white from her grip on the porch rail. "I was naïve and foolish. It was nothing but misguided hero worship."

Logan flinched, an unexpected pain spearing his chest. He'd spent so much time in the past trying to reason the idea with her. Trying to get her to understand what she felt for him was nothing more than a crush. That, at four years her senior, he was easy to look up to and become infatuated with.

But, as she'd grown, he'd had to work harder at talking himself into believing it, too. And on that ride home from the pool hall the night of her nineteenth birthday, she'd turned to him, put her hands on him and touched that beautiful mouth of hers to his.

And, heaven help him, he'd given in. Over and over again during the next two months. Helpless to put a stop to it. Not even wanting to.

She'd sent his self-control up in flames more times than he cared to remember. Had continued to push for more until he was so desperate not to lose her altogether that he gave in whenever she wanted.

Logan squeezed his eyes shut. He should've been more responsible back then. Wiser. Shouldn't have blindly accepted her word that she'd been protected. That she'd taken care of things.

He learned later she deliberately hadn't. And, as a result, they'd made a daughter then lost her. He'd almost lost Amy, too. All because of her selfish obsession.

"But you didn't leave it at that," he gritted, facing her. "You had to have your way."

"I never meant to hurt you." Her face flushed. "Not then and not now. As hard as it is to believe, that's God's honest truth."

"We both have regrets, Amy." He sighed and shook his head. "You were so young. You think that sits well with me? That I didn't step up? Put a stop to things?"

She smiled. It was small. A joyless tilt. "I knew what I was doing, Logan. Even at nineteen. And even if you were my first."

"I was never interested in being your first."

"I know. You wanted to stay friends. Wanted me to grow up. Live and learn." She released the rail, wrapping her arms around her middle. "Well, I have. I'm not that girl anymore. I've learned and I won't ever be like her again."

He clenched his eyes shut. She was right. He'd wanted to wait. Had spent so much time waiting. Waiting for her to mature. Waiting to see if her adoration grew into something real. Something he could trust. Her friendship had been too important for him to risk it.

"I really and truly thought back then that all you needed was a little push," she said. "That if I could show you how I felt, you'd understand and feel the same. That

you'd want the same things and I could make you happy."
A humorless laugh burst from her. "It was such a stupid
teenage thing to do. So ridiculous. And you called me on
it. Do you remember what you said to me?" she asked.
"When I told you I was glad I'd gotten pregnant? That
it'd been my intention?"

His stomach roiled, a roaring sounding in his ears.

"You told me I was selfish. That I had a selfish obsession."

"I was angry." Dragging his tongue from the dry roof
of his mouth, he said, "I should've been less blunt. You
were so young—"

"But it was the truth, wasn't it?" She kneaded her
nape with both hands. "I was selfish and obsessed. I
never had a clue how to be a real friend." She shook her
head. "But that was the best lesson I ever learned. I've
learned how to be a good friend, Logan. I have. And I
finally did the right thing and filed. You don't have to
pay for my mistake anymore."

A mistake. Their daughter a mistake. Their marriage
a mista—

"Marrying you was not a mistake," he rasped. "I
chose to make you promises and I intend to keep them."

"That's my Logan," she whispered. Her fingertips
rose, bumping gently across the creases on his forehead
and following the hard line of his jaw. "Always doing
the right thing. The honest, honorable thing. That's how
you got into this mess to begin with." She leaned in, her
breasts brushing his chest. "We both have a chance to
get out of this. To get our lives back. All you have to
do is sign."

He caught her wrists and pressed a kiss to her palms.

"I vowed to take care of you and love you every day of my life. I don't break my promises."

She stilled, her expression lifting. "And do you? Love me?"

He eased his hold on her when the dig of fragile bone hit his flesh. "You were the best friend I'd ever had. I've always cared for you."

"That's not what I'm asking." She stepped closer, the heat in her eyes burning into him. "You said you swore to love me. What does that mean to you?"

He clamped his jaw so tight he thought his teeth would shatter. *Damn words*. Every time he was near her, they jumbled up. They tied together in knots, clogging his throat and never escaping the way he intended. But not this time.

This one time, the bastards were sharp, clean and at the ready. And, he had no clue if they were the ones she wanted to hear.

"Tell me, Logan." Her voice firmed. "What does loving me mean to you?"

"It means you have my loyalty. My fidelity and protection. And my support."

Her face fell. The spark in her eyes faded, her long lashes swooping down and masking them. She placed her hand on his chest. Her favorite spot. The place she'd always clung to the hardest whenever he'd moved into her. Over her. The spot she'd nuzzled her cheek against every time he'd held her.

"Those are all very important things," she said. "Very practical things. But what about your heart?"

His heart. Something so much weaker than his head. Erratic. Just like his mother's when she'd abandoned her family for some other man. Like his father's when he'd failed to function for months after she'd left. And like Amy's all those years ago when she'd tempted him down a path he'd never meant to travel.

There were no sure things or guaranteed happy endings in life. Just chance and disappointment. Loyalty was much more tangible and steadfast.

Logan shook his head. "Hearts are unpredictable. Untrustworthy. The kind of love you're asking for doesn't exist, Amy. It's just some notion thrown into kids' fairy tales."

Releasing her wrists, he smoothed his hands around her back, pulling her closer and trying not to plead. "I don't break my promises. I'm offering you something real. Something you can depend on. Something we've both already sworn to each other."

She straightened. That beautiful back of hers drew up into a proud tilt against his palms, breasts thrusting and stubborn chin jutting.

"That all sounds so nice," she said. "But I'm not tying either of us to a vow we made as a result of my stupid teenage lie."

"Amy—"

"You loved me as a friend. A young friend that just happened to grow up on the same ranch as you. I should have recognized that a long time ago." She stepped back and trailed her hands from him. "I won't take anything more from you. And I won't let you sacrifice anything more for me. If I did, I'd be no more of a woman now than I was at nineteen."

Logan's gut roiled. So, she'd leave instead. He wouldn't have her at all and it would amount to nothing more than a mistake. Another regret.

"I'm sorry, Logan," she whispered. "More sorry than you'll ever know."

He clenched his teeth, half-afraid they'd crumble, and studied the tense curve of her jaw. They'd both always been hardheaded and Amy could hold out longer than anyone. But he'd never known her to be able to walk away from a challenge.

"It's one thing to say it," he said. "Why don't you show me, instead?"

She glanced at him, features clouding.

"Stay," he said. "Do right by your family. Do right by me."

She shook her head. "It's too late for that."

"No. That's just your excuse." He shoved away from the porch rail and moved to the door, turning to say, "You haven't changed. Don't know a thing about loyalty. You're no different now than you were back then. The girl that stood right in front of me and lied to get her way is the same woman that's turning her back on her family now. And I'm your family, too, Amy. You worked hard to snag me. You oughta have the guts to stick it out."

She flinched, body stiffening and face paling.

He watched. Waited. Then forced himself to turn on his heel and jerk open the door.

"Wait."

He froze, the sweet sound of her voice sweeping over him. Turning, he watched her pick at her pants leg and shift from foot to foot. She came to a decision, stilling and drawing to her full height.

"I'll stay," she whispered. "Long enough to work with Thunder."

"Absolutely not." Logan held up a hand. "That horse is dangerous."

"I can help him. You know I can."

"Neither one of us knows that for sure, Amy." He blew out a breath in frustration. "You could get hurt. Badly."

"Then help me."

He hesitated. If he refused, there was a good chance she'd leave or, worse yet, put herself in even more danger by trying to work with the horse on the sly. But his throat tightened at the thought of her approaching the maddened stallion.

She interpreted his silence as agreement.

"So it's settled. I'll stay. Just until it's time for me to take up the post in Michigan. I'll work with Thunder and help ease Mama into the idea of the move. But as for us," she said, shaking her head, "I can't stay in this marriage, Logan. It's not good for either of us. We'd both be miserable."

"What makes you so sure?" His muscles tightened, a wave of nausea flooding through him. "Is there someone else?"

"No," she stated firmly.

He forced the next question past his constricted throat. "You're not still hoping for another baby, are you?"

She recoiled, fear flooding her features, and shook her head.

He stepped forward and cradled her arms. "I'm sorry, Amy. I know how hard it was for you to accept that you can't have any more children. But after Sara—" he swallowed hard, eyeing her pale cheeks "—I have no desire to have another child, either. So what's to stop us? It'll keep the family together." He rubbed his thumbs gently over her skin. "Plenty of marriages have been based on a lot less than the friendship we have."

"Had," she stressed, moving away. "We lost our friendship along with everything else. And I won't stay in a marriage out of duty."

"That's a damn sight better than throwing it away." He spun the ring on his finger with jerky movements of his thumb.

Amy kicked off her shoes, slamming the loose heel against the porch rail to break it off, then did the same with the other and rolled up her pants legs.

"What are you doing?"

"Getting started," she said, slipping her shoes back on and scooping up the beer bottle. "The sooner I begin helping Thunder, the better."

She made her way down the porch steps, plucking the pins from her hair with one hand as she went and combing through the long, dark waves with her fingers.

"It's too cold out, Amy." He fell in line behind her, body tightening with a surge of heat at the supple sway of her hips. "Come back inside and get a good night's sleep. It'll wait 'til morning."

"No time like the present."

And that was it. That was all he got before she tipped up the beer and quickened her step, raven hair swinging as she disappeared into the dark night.

Logan stopped, rammed his hands into the pockets of his jeans and headed back to the house. *Stubborn, hardheaded woman.* Only Amy would camp out in a stable in the dead of night, freezing her tail off. Hell if he'd encourage her.

He took long strides across the lawn only to halt at

the foot of the stairs. He should let her go. Walk away. It was the sane, sensible thing to do.

And he almost did. Almost kept right on going. Into the house and an empty bed. Away from Amy. Away from the mess of their marriage. Only, his legs wouldn't budge.

"Damn."

Logan spun back around and followed the same path Amy had taken, moving swiftly across the field toward the stable.

Chapter Five

"She's dead."

Amy inhaled, her peaceful hold on sleep slipping with the intrusive whisper.

"Nah," a second voice declared. "She just breathed, see?"

"No, she didn't. She freezed to death."

That was Jayden. The uncertain tremor and concern in his voice gave it away.

A small hand poked Amy's chest and the warm presence of two small bodies closed in at her sides. Her mouth twitched. She kept her eyes shut and shifted on the stable floor, pressing deeper into the heat at her back, reluctant to release her relaxed state.

A strong hand flexed on her hip. Amy stilled, her stomach flipping as she recognized the familiar strength at her back.

Last night, Logan had tried his best to talk her into going back inside but she'd been determined to stay by Thunder's stall. The stallion had been left alone too long, cooped up away from everyone. She couldn't stand the thought of him spending another night in isolation. Instead, she'd settled on the cold stable floor, keeping a vigilant eye on Thunder.

She'd hoped Thunder would relax after getting used to her scent again. Had thought it might even help him settle down and find comfort in having someone close. It'd worked to a certain extent. Even though Thunder had started his usual intimidation tactics when they'd arrived at his stall, he'd eventually quieted down after a couple of hours. After which, she must have fallen asleep.

Logan, true to his word, had stayed at her side, gathering her against him and throwing a blanket over them. And, as usual, she'd settled right back into his arms. Even in her sleep.

"If she's dead, then that means Uncle Logan's dead, too." Kayden's whisper tickled her ear. "He was with her. And he ain't moving neither."

"Uh-uh," Jayden argued. "If Aunt Amy's dead, it's 'cuz she froze to death. But Uncle Logan wouldn't die 'cuz men don't get cold."

Logan's chest shook. His gentle breaths of silent laughter ruffled her hair. Apparently, he was playing along, too.

"I know how to check," Kayden said.

Amy cringed as the tip of Kayden's tiny finger jerked her eyelid up, making her eye roll with discomfort. He released it and sat back with a sigh.

"Yep," Kayden said sadly. "She's dead."

"Do something." Jayden's voice turned anxious.

"What do you want me to do?" Kayden's tone was long-suffering.

"Give her CRP."

"What?"

"CRP," Jayden said. "You know? Blow air in her mouth."

Okay. That was enough playing along. Amy opened her eyes.

Kayden sucked in a mouthful of air, held it with puffed cheeks and leaned forward.

Amy held him off with a hand. "That's not necessary, Kay—"

The sharp slam of Thunder's hoof against the stall door sounded, an earsplitting crack of wood cutting through the air and causing them all to jump. Logan's arms shot out, snagging the boys close. He bundled them all together and rolled over, pressing against the wall and covering them.

"What's happening?" Jayden cried, his arms tight around Amy's neck.

"That mean horse is trying to stomp on us." Kayden burrowed his blond head into her middle.

"No." Logan's voice, calm and soothing, rumbled at her back. "He's just letting us know he wants his space."

Thunder's assault on the stall door ceased. Logan tensed, holding them all tight in the wake of the silence, then eased back. He stood and tugged them, each in turn, to their feet.

"Land sakes, what have the boys done now?"

Betty stood in the stable entrance, Traci at her side, and eyed the twins.

"Nothing," Amy said hastily. "Thunder's being rowdy is all."

"Rowdy's an understatement," Logan said, frowning. "He's about to take that door down. We need to turn him out so I can work on it. Don't want to chance him breaking it down tonight."

"He wants out," Jayden murmured.

His sad eyes lingered on Thunder. He took a hesitant step toward the stall. Thunder resumed kicking, his hooves slamming against the stall walls and echoing around the stable.

Logan jumped in front of Jayden and examined the door for damage. "We're about to turn him out, buddy."

"Why can't we let him out *now*?" Jayden slipped between Logan's parted legs, stretching up on his toes and reaching for the latch on the stall.

"No, Jayden." Logan spun him gently toward Betty. "You leave this to me and keep your distance from him. He's dangerous."

"But—"

"No buts. Thunder's wild when he's loose. He needs to be fenced in." He ruffled Jayden's blond hair and nudged him toward the door. "You and Kayden can watch Thunder all you want once we turn him out. For now, you keep out of the way."

Jayden glanced up at Amy, his chin trembling and blue eyes glistening. "He doesn't like it in there. He wants out."

Amy's chest tightened. She patted his cheek and smiled. "I know he does. And we're going to let him out for some fresh air soon."

"Well, in that case, you boys go on in and get some breakfast," Betty said. "Give Logan and Amy time to get a handle on Thunder, then you can come back out to watch later on."

Kayden grumbled on his way past Betty and Jayden trudged behind but both boys picked up their pace at hearing pancakes and bacon were waiting on them.

"Pop told me he found the two of you out here with Thunder last night," Betty said. "We got worried when you didn't show back up." She tilted her head at Amy, expression cautious. "I guess this means you changed your mind about working with Thunder?"

Amy nodded. "I don't know how much progress I'll make with the little time I have but I promised Logan I'd give it a shot while I'm here."

Betty glanced at Logan. "I'm glad to hear that."

Logan ducked his head and resumed examining Thunder's stall.

"I brought a pancake and bacon sandwich out for each of you." Betty smiled, placing two foiled bundles in Amy's hands. "Figured if y'all were gung ho to stay out here all night, you wouldn't take a break long enough to eat this morning. The hands were wolfing them down so fast, I didn't think there'd be any left by the time you did get around to coming in."

The thick weight of the packages warmed Amy's palms and the sweet aroma caused her stomach to growl. The rumble was loud and long, triggering Logan's deep chuckle at her back and a giggle from Traci.

Amy joined them, the laughter lifting her spirits. For a moment, it felt like home again. The way it used to before things went so bad. When the ranch was full of comforts, family and laughter. A time when she'd never wanted to leave.

"Take a few minutes to eat before you start working," Betty said. "You can't make it through a long day on no sleep and an empty stomach."

Betty smiled but her eyes were puffy. Dark circles hovered beneath them and a red tinge lined her lashes.

Amy winced, a lump rising in her throat. Betty had probably stayed up half the night, too. Worrying and weeping. And she'd been the cause of it.

"Thank you, Mama." Amy hugged her close, murmuring near her ear, "I'm not going anywhere yet, you know?"

Betty sighed, squeezing her tight. "I know. I'm glad to have you home for however long you're able to stay." She pulled back and smiled. "I'm happy about your new job and I'll help in whatever way I can. For now, let's just have a great Christmas together, okay?"

Amy grinned, the pressure easing in her chest. "Yes, ma'am."

Betty looked at Logan. "Dominic and Pop said they'd handle the trail rides for you today. So make sure you eat, too, before getting started."

Logan dipped his head and winked. "Yes ma'am."

Betty left, calling over her shoulder, "I gotta get back to the kitchen. Sun's coming up and there's a hungry crowd of guests that needs to be fed."

Amy tugged at Traci's arm as she turned to leave. "You're still gonna help me out with Thunder, right?"

Traci's brows rose. "Do you want me to?"

"Of course. I wouldn't have it any other way." Amy placed the foiled sandwiches in Traci's hand. "Can you do me a favor and hold on to these? I need to change out of these clothes before we get started, then you can watch me work on getting Thunder out of the stall." She laughed. "Or, at least, try getting him out. Do you think you can round up a couple sticks and strings? We'll need a rope, too."

Traci beamed. "No problem."

Amy changed into a gray hoodie, jeans and boots then joined Logan and Traci outside. The strong morning sun had broken out above the horizon and burned off the frost from last night. The air turned warmer and the wind less fierce. Amy tilted her head back and pushed up her sleeves, absorbing the heat.

Figured. Georgia weather was unpredictable at best. It could be thirty degrees at night then spring back to seventy by noon. She'd learned a long time ago to just take it as it came.

She, Logan and Traci took up residence on the white fence lining the paddock. They lingered over the sweet and salty breakfast Betty had provided, watching the horses stroll across the dormant brown grass of the fields. The pleasant chatter of guests sounded and, soon, Raintree's grounds were speckled with visitors, all soaking up the pleasant late–November day.

After eating, Logan brought the hose around and they scrubbed their hands under the spray, cleaning the traces of grease and sweet aroma of the sandwiches away. The fewer strange smells introduced to Thunder, the better.

Amy brought the hose to her mouth, swallowing a few gulps of the water, the metallic taste of the nozzle clinging to her tongue. Logan followed suit, splashing the spray over his face and rasping his palms over the stubble lining his jaw. The thick muscles of his shoulders and back rippled beneath the tight pull of his shirt with each movement.

Amy's palms itched at the display, a deep longing to smooth her hands over his broad shoulders and weave her fingers through the dark waves of his hair overwhelming her. She turned away and faced Traci.

"Did you round up everything?"

"Yep." Traci handed the items to her. "Rope, sticks and strings, just like you asked for."

Amy thanked her and attached strings to two of the training sticks.

"You ready?" Logan asked, turning off the faucet and shaking his hands dry.

Amy nodded, handed Logan the rope and one of the sticks then led the way into the stable. Her heart tripped in her chest.

A finger threaded through her back belt loop and tugged. She stopped and looked over her shoulder. Logan's eyes peered into hers, the sensual curve of his lips pressing into a firm line.

"Go easy, Amy," he said.

She swallowed hard, ignoring the warm flutter in her belly, and walked to the back of the stable to stand in front of Thunder's stall. The stallion pinned his ears and tossed his head back, nostrils flaring on sharp pulls of air.

Amy's thighs trembled. The shaking traveled down her knees to her shins, leaving her lower half weak and unstable.

"Easy," Logan repeated.

He stood a few feet away, a tic appearing in his jaw. Traci hovered behind him.

Amy waited as Logan prepared his rope, studying the movements of his strong hands. The thick, twisted fibers seemed like such a weak support against a frightened, thousand-pound animal. She closed her eyes and placed her hand on the latch of Thunder's stall.

LOGAN MOVED CLOSE to the stall, keeping an eye on Thunder as he whipped the rope overhead and lassoed him. The stallion cried and kicked the wall with his back hooves, thrashing against the pull of the rope.

"It's okay, boy," Amy murmured.

Thunder stopped at the sound of her voice, pinned his ears back and pawed the ground. Logan's throat closed.

"Go wait for us outside, Traci." Logan firmed his hold on the rope, then nodded after Traci left. "Let him out."

Amy unlatched the stall and pulled it open, raising her arms and directing Thunder's feet toward the exit. The stallion backed away, jerking wildly, but eventually exited with her encouragement.

It took several minutes to maneuver Thunder out of the stable and into the round pen. Logan removed the rope and let him buck around the pen until he settled down and drew to a halt on one side.

Amy moved toward the entrance of the pen, her tender expression causing Logan's mouth to run dry.

"He's not like you remember, Amy. He's aggressive now. Likes to dive and bite. You have to start hard and end hard." Logan lifted his training stick, jiggling the string and motioning toward hers. "Use that thing on him if you need to."

She frowned. "I've never whipped a horse and I won't start now."

Logan shook his head. "I've never done it, either. But the last time I tried to work with him, he almost forced me into a position where I had no choice."

"This time will be different," she said, walking to the gate.

He bit back a curse. "How you figure?"

She stopped and faced him. "Because you have help. We're doing this together."

Together. Logan glanced away, focusing on Thunder

and ignoring the pleasurable tingle sweeping through him. There was no room for distractions in that pen.

He cleared his throat. "We start hard and we end hard."

Amy opened the gate and they entered, walking to the center of the round pen. Thunder pinned his ears and pawed the ground, dipping his head and snaking it from side to side as if to attack. Logan immediately threw his left hand up and whipped his training stick behind Thunder's heels, lashing the ground with the string.

"Move," he shouted.

Thunder started then ran left, making it halfway around the pen before he stopped. Amy stepped in, striking her stick against the ground behind him and forcing him forward. Thunder balked, rearing and spinning his back to her.

Amy slapped the ground with the stick again, regaining Thunder's attention. She pointed in the air and shouted, "Right."

Thunder complied, running around the curve of the pen, but stopped again. He laid back his ears again and made to charge.

Logan ran him back, thrashing the ground with his stick and yelling, "Move!"

They continued the tactics, shouting commands and running Thunder around the pen until he began to respond.

"Good boy," Amy praised, easing off when Thunder obeyed a request the first time it was issued.

Logan returned to her side. They stood still, breathing hard and watching Thunder trot around the pen.

"He's doing good, huh?" Traci called from the other side of the fence.

Amy's eyes followed Thunder's progress. "Looks that way." She turned, glancing up at him with excitement. "It's an improvement, right?"

Logan smiled. "Yeah. But he still has a long way to go." He took a step back but stayed close to her side. "When he comes around, ask him to face you. See if he'll give you both eyes."

Amy did as instructed, dropping her arms and maintaining her stance. Thunder drew to a halt, faced her and pricked his ears forward.

"Remember me, beautiful?" she asked.

Thunder huffed and ducked his head.

Amy took a step forward. "It's okay, boy." Then another.

Thunder licked his lips and Amy moved close. She murmured phrases of affection and rubbed his forehead.

"Can we try to saddle him now?" Traci asked.

"Not yet," Logan said. "This is just the first step. It'll take a lot of attention and time."

Traci eased closer to the fence, eyes glued to Amy's actions. Thunder relaxed even more with each of Amy's touches and eventually, he allowed Amy to smooth her palm over his neck. He leaned into her hand, tilting his head slightly when she scratched a favorable spot.

Amy giggled and smiled. "He might put up a hard front but he's still a softie underneath." She crossed carefully to Thunder's other side and continued the tender touches. "You like getting attention. Huh, handsome?"

A low rumble of pleasure sounded in Thunder's throat and he leaned closer to Amy.

Logan chuckled. She was good with a horse. Always had been.

"Ready to give him his space?" Logan opened the gate.

Amy nodded and they exited the round pen.

"You're stopping?" Traci's brows furrowed as she moved to Amy's side.

"Yeah," Logan said. "Horses learn as much from the release of pressure as they do when you exert it."

"Thunder's worked hard and he's been cooped up in that stall for a long time." Amy squinted against the afternoon sun, shielding her eyes with her hand. "He deserves a chance to burn off some energy."

As if on cue, Thunder cried and tore around the pen. His black mane rippled and clods of dirt sprayed from his hooves on every pass.

"How's the training going?"

Logan turned to find Cissy strolling toward them. The boys skipped ahead of her, their blue eyes bright and excited.

"You might want the boys to stay back, Cissy," Logan said. "He's making progress, but he's still dangerous."

Cissy hurried forward and pinched the boys' shirts, tugging them away a few feet. The boys grumbled and strained against her hold, gazes flicking expectantly from Thunder to Amy.

"He seems angry today," Cissy said.

"No more than usual. They've done wonders with him already," Traci said, grabbing the railing as if preparing to duck down. She glanced at Amy. "Want me to help you run him the next round?"

"Not yet." Amy threw out a hand. "Stay there. And help Cissy keep the boys still."

Thunder noticed the onlookers, his eyes growing wild and his cries increasing.

"He just wants out," Jayden said, pulling agains Cissy's hold.

"Shhh." Cissy tapped a finger against her mouth. "Amy and Logan are helping him. You have to be quiet if you want to stay."

Logan tensed, shifting from one boot to the other, and kept an eye on Thunder. The stallion remained at the opposite end of the enclosure, bucking and rearing. Each kick of his hooves against the fence clanged louder than the one before it.

The muscles of his neck and chest stood out in sharp relief. His midnight hide gleamed almost blue in the sun. The long black strands of his mane and tail flew in strong arcs with each of his head tosses and kicks.

"It's okay, boy," Amy soothed, slipping back through the fence.

"Amy," Logan said. "Wait." He caught her wrist and tugged. "He's too worked up."

"I'll be fine," she whispered, pulling away.

She straightened and lifted a hand. The shiny length of her raven hair rippled across her back as she approached the center of the pen with graceful ease. The stallion backed up, calming slightly at the sight of her.

Logan's eyes clung to them, admiration surging through him. A crack of laughter rang out from a neighboring field. Two guests cackled from their saddles as their friend struggled to mount his horse with a ranch hand's assistance. Thunder bucked. His hooves struck with violent smacks against the fencing again.

"Go ahead, boy," Amy said. "Kick all that steam out."

The click and creak of the paddock gate rang out.

"No, Jayden!" Cissy shouted.

Logan spun, eyes shooting to the gate. Jayden clung to the top of it, releasing the latch and swaying as it swung open. Cissy ran toward Jayden as fast as the girth of her belly allowed, stumbling over the ground and falling hard to her hands and knees.

Hooves pounded at Logan's back, increasing in intensity and heading straight for Jayden and Cissy. Logan shoved away from the fence and sprinted toward them.

"Move, Amy," he yelled, racing past.

Logan shoved the gate as he ran, thrusting Jayden out of Thunder's path and barely rolling Cissy out of the way as Thunder charged. The stallion barreled past, eyes wild and lips drawn, kicking up a spray of dirt. It stung Logan's eyes, caking his lashes and obscuring his vision. He rubbed the back of his arm across his face and blinked hard.

Shrieks and yelps from the guests shattered the cheerful atmosphere as the startled stallion darted wildly in different directions, alarming the other horses and causing them to bolt. One of the horses saddled up for the next trail ride reared. The man on his back toppled off and slammed to the ground.

Logan knelt at Cissy's side and cradled her against him. She sat up with his assistance, chest rising and falling on ragged breaths.

"Are you okay?" Amy asked, rushing over and placing a hand to the curve of Cissy's belly.

Cissy nodded and pushed to her feet. "I'm fine."

"Don't force it," Logan said, supporting her arms. "Sit for a minute."

"I'm okay, really," Cissy said. She tried for a smile. "Just clumsy nowadays." Her blue eyes darted beyond Logan's shoulder, voice trembling. "Jayden?"

Logan glanced toward the gate. Traci stood beside it, hugging both crying boys against her legs.

"Are they okay?" Logan called out.

Traci nodded. "They're fine."

The yells from guests continued. Confused by the crowds, Thunder gathered speed and leapt over a fence into an adjoining pasture, galloping through groups of horses. They scattered and took off in all directions.

"Get him," Cissy gasped, waving a hand in Thunder's direction. "Before he hurts someone else."

Amy spun and took off. Logan tore his eyes from Amy and tightened his hold on Cissy's arms. He skimmed his gaze down her length once more for injuries. There were none visible aside from the scrapes on her hands.

"Go," Cissy insisted, patting his chest. "I'm fine. Go help Amy."

"Aunt Cissy?" Kayden ran to her side and reached a hand up to her belly.

Logan grabbed it and tugged the boy around to face him. "You and your brother go straight to the house and tell Mrs. Betty she's needed down here right away."

Kayden blinked, blue eyes darting over the chaotic fields surrounding them.

"Kayden." Logan shook him. "Do you hear me?"

"Yes, sir." He motioned to his brother and they ran toward the safety of the main house.

"Traci, stay with Cissy," he said. "You're not to leave her side until your mom gets here. Understand?"

Traci nodded and wrapped an arm around Cissy. Logan hesitated, stomach dropping as Amy gained more distance.

Cissy shoved at his chest. "I'm fine. Go."

Logan scrambled around in the dirt for the rope. Fisting it, he tore off after Amy.

She was ahead of him, climbing over the fence. Logan ran faster, slowing as he approached the pasture Amy had entered. Thunder paced at one end, tossing his head and eyeing the chaotic movements of guests. Amy stood several feet away, motionless, with her right side facing Thunder.

Logan froze. Thunder was scared and confused. And Amy would be no match for a thousand-pound animal that fought to protect itself. If Thunder felt threatened enough to attack...

She's dead.

Logan flinched. Jayden's innocent whisper from earlier returned, spearing his gut and reverberating in his skull.

His hands shook. Exactly as they had years ago. The night he'd sat beside Amy's hospital bed, watching her work her way silently through the dark delivery of their stillborn daughter. Unable to help her. And unable to save their baby girl.

She's dead.

Logan's heart slammed against his ribs, his eyes blurring. "Get out of there, Amy. Let me handle it."

She glanced at Thunder and walked a few steps away from him. "Just give him a minute."

Logan frowned and studied her determined expression. She wasn't leaving that pasture and there was no way he could drag her out without spooking Thunder even more.

Thunder eyed Amy, jerking his head and shuffling from side to side. Amy moved further away, stopped then murmured words of affection.

They watched and waited. After several restless movements, Thunder stilled and took a hesitant step toward her.

She walked a few more steps, slowing as Thunder approached and halted calmly at her side. Amy reached out, stroked Thunder's forehead with the back of her hand and eased away. She applied and removed her touch on both sides of the stallion, speaking to him in soothing tones.

A few minutes later, she walked away again. Thunder followed, stepping behind her and waiting for direction. Logan sighed as Amy stroked Thunder's forehead with one hand and held her left side with the other. A small amount of blood seeped through her shirt.

"You're hurt," he rasped, stomach dropping to his knees.

"It's only a scratch." She glanced at the cut then him. "A nail caught me when I was going over the fence."

Logan held her stare, shoulders sagging with relief. The wind rifled through the trees lining the pasture, scattering rust-colored leaves around the fence and sweeping over them in a quiet whisper. Thunder leaned further into Amy's soothing touch and dropped his head.

"Good boy." Amy gently scratched Thunder's neck, her gaze lingering on Logan's mouth. "I think we can work with this."

Logan's chest tightened, heat buzzing in his blood at her coy grin. She looked so much like she used to. Vibrant and strong. Eager to gain his approval. Scaring him with her impulsive actions and impressing him in equal measure.

He smiled. "We're still a helluva team, yeah?"

"The best one around," she said.

It all rushed in at once. The flirtatious gleam in her eye and confident tilt of her chin. The excitement lighting her expression. Every bit of her as wild and unpredictable as that horse she gentled.

Logan's fist tightened around the rope in his hand. He'd never wanted her so much. Had never been more drawn to her. Or, so terrified.

Chapter Six

"I told him, I'm fine," Cissy grumbled.

She shifted beneath the stark, white sheet covering the exam table and huffed. A strand of blond hair slipped down over her eyes. Cissy batted it back only for it to fall again.

Amy smiled. She reached out from her seat beside the exam table and tucked it behind Cissy's ear.

"I compromise on a lot, Cissy," Dominic said, pausing his restless movements and leveling a stern look on her. "But I'm not taking any chances with this."

Amy winced. It was a wonder Dominic hadn't worn a hole in the floor with the amount of pacing he'd undertaken over the past hour. At this rate, he'd be in a hospital bed alongside Cissy for high blood pressure.

Cissy sighed. "There's no winning with Dominic when he's in this mood."

Amy smiled and squeezed Cissy's hand. She glanced at Logan hovering in the corner on the other side of the room. He crossed his arms over his broad chest and planted his feet wider apart. There was never any winning with him, either. Both Slade men could bow their back up better than a bull. Dominic had proved as much a few hours earlier.

After successfully moving Thunder back to his stall, Amy and Logan had returned to the main house to find Dominic bundling Cissy into his truck to make the drive to the nearest hospital. Amy and Logan followed close behind in Logan's truck, leaving the boys in Betty's care.

They'd ended up spending the afternoon and early evening waiting in the emergency room near the revolving entry doors. Dominic's agitation had grown with each passing hour and remained after they were ushered into an exam room then to an ultrasound lab. He stopped pacing momentarily and crossed the small room to touch a kiss to Cissy's forehead. "There's no way we're leaving here until I know my girls are safe." His voice lowered and he placed a hand on her belly. "All of them."

Logan shifted, dragging a hand over his face and closing his eyes. The dark stubble across his chiseled jaw matched the black night that had fallen outside. His broad shoulders tensed and he maintained his silence.

Amy's chest ached. She'd only ever seen him this anxious once before. When she'd been the one in the hospital bed and they'd shared the same worry as Dominic and Cissy. And the outcome had been exactly as they'd feared.

Logan caught her eyes on him. He drew his head back, composed his features and turned to stare at the open doorway. She couldn't blame him. This was the last place she wanted to be, too.

Amy slipped a hand under her sweater to rub the throbbing cut on her side, careful not to dislodge the bandage covering it. A warm dampness met her fingertips and she stifled a wince. It'd been a close call earlier but they'd all been lucky. She just hoped their luck for the day continued a little longer.

A nurse swept into the room and closed the door behind her. "Sorry for the long wait." She smiled with apology and sat on a stool by the exam table, tugging a latex glove on each hand with a snap. "It's been a busy night."

Amy's gut churned and sweat broke out across her brow.

"Let's have a look at these beautiful babies and make sure they're comfortable," the nurse said.

Logan squeezed Dominic's shoulder and strolled to the door. He hovered on the threshold, looking expectantly in Amy's direction.

"We'll wait outside," Amy said, releasing Cissy's hand.

"No." Cissy grabbed the sleeve of her sweater. "Please stay."

Her chin trembled but she grinned and held up her other hand which held Dominic's. She wiggled it and laughed nervously.

"What with the boys, I've gotten used to having both hands full," Cissy said. "It's more comforting."

Amy hesitated at the fear shadowing Cissy's eyes. She knew how it felt to lie on a bed waiting for the world to crumble. To hear your worst nightmare as a mother spoken out loud by a stranger.

Amy sighed, forcing a small smile and taking Cissy's hand again.

Logan shifted restlessly at the exit. "Amy—"

"I'm staying, Logan."

He frowned but didn't argue, leaving and shutting the door behind him.

"Thank you for staying," Cissy whispered.

The nurse tugged the hem of Cissy's hospital gown from underneath the cover and Dominic tucked the sheet around the underside of her bare belly.

"I told my husband this wasn't necessary." Cissy laughed nervously. "It really wasn't that hard of a fall, and I feel perfectly fine."

The nurse smiled and rolled closer on the stool, squeezing a glob of jelly onto Cissy's protruding middle.

"It never hurts to double-check," she said. "Besides—" she winked at Dominic "—I think this proud papa will rest easier knowing all of you are okay."

Dominic nodded, jaw clenching and dark eyes worried. Amy tightened her hand around Cissy's and did her best to put on a calm front.

The next few minutes stretched on for an eternity as the nurse moved the probe over Cissy's belly. She searched around then hovered in one spot. A strong throb pulsated around the room, evoking a heavy sigh of relief from Dominic. Locating the second heartbeat, the nurse eased back on the stool to give them all an unobstructed view of the monitor.

"There," she said. "You can relax. Mom and babies are safe and comfortable."

Dominic's smile stretched wide.

The nurse packed up the equipment and wiped Cissy's skin clean, pausing on her way out to say, "You two better get plenty of rest. The opportunity will be gone in a couple months."

Dominic chuckled. He bent, showering kisses all over Cissy's belly, then cradled her face in his big palms and touched a tender kiss to her lips.

The bittersweetness of the sight warmed Amy's chest

and tears welled in her eyes. She dropped her gaze, the cut on her side throbbing stronger than ever.

Cissy laughed. "Can we go home now?"

"Yep." Dominic straightened. "I'll help you get dressed and we'll check out."

Amy's skin heated beneath the weight of Dominic's scrutiny.

"Amy?" Dominic's warm palm touched her arm. "Why don't you and Logan head back home? It's been a long day for y'all, too."

Amy nodded.

"Do you mind checking on the boys for us when you get back?" Cissy asked.

"I'd be glad to."

Amy moved to the door, pressing a fingertip to the corner of each eye as she turned away. Dominic's heavy tread sounded behind her.

"Thanks, Ames," he said, pecking a kiss to her cheek. "Thank Logan for me, too, okay?"

Amy left and joined Logan in the hall.

"The babies are fine," she said. "And so is Cissy."

Logan released a heavy breath. He shoved away from the wall and stepped close. His dark eyes hovered on her face. He swept the pad of his thumb over the wetness lining her lower lashes.

Drawing his hand away, he rubbed his thumb and forefinger together and his mouth drew into a tight line. "Let's get outta here."

His big hand engulfed hers and squeezed, pulling her to the exit.

The drive home was silent. Only the sporadic clicking of the truck's blinker and jingle of keys hanging from the ignition filled the cab. Logan squeezed Amy's hand for the length of the ride, releasing it to change gears or navigate a turn then clasping it tight again.

They pulled to a stop in front of the main house. The truck's headlights flooded the front porch, highlighting the boys and Betty huddled on the steps under a blanket.

"Their little butts should be in bed." Logan cut the engine and thrust the door open.

"Don't be so hard on them. They had good intentions."

Amy sighed at his glower. She trailed Logan to the porch, wincing as the boys' eyes widened up at him. They scrunched together, tugging the blanket up over their heads.

"What are you two still doing up?" Logan pulled the cover down.

"They wanted to wait for Cissy to get home." Betty stood and ran the back of her hand across her forehead. "We've all been worried. But, at least, we've been able to rest a little easier since Dominic called from the hospital to say they'd be on the way back soon."

"Well, that'll take some time, yet," Logan said. "Everything's fine. There's no need to wait." He steered Betty toward the door. "Take a break and put your feet up. We'll look after the boys."

Betty nodded gratefully, saying over her shoulder, "Pop and Traci are still out in the stables. They had a lot of horses to calm down but they should be in soon."

Logan waited as the door closed behind Betty, then glared down at the boys.

"Do you have any idea how much chaos you created this afternoon?"

Kayden sat up, face twisting. "Uh-uh. Don't look at me, Uncle Logan. I ain't do it this time. It was all Jay—"

"You." Logan snapped his fingers at Kayden, then pointed to the door. "Bed. Now."

Kayden clamped his mouth shut, jumped to his feet and scurried inside.

"Hate to say it," Logan murmured, "but Kayden's right this time." He narrowed his eyes on Jayden. "What were you thinking, Jayden? This is the kinda thing I'd expect from your brother. Not from you."

Jayden's lips quivered. "I wanted to—"

"Didn't I tell you to keep your distance from Thunder and let us handle it?" Logan shook his head. "I told you he gets wild when he's let loose. And, yet, you did the exact opposite of what I told you to do."

Jayden's eyes flooded, big tears spilling over his lashes and streaming down his cheeks.

"But he was sad," Jayden whispered. "He wanted out—"

"He's not sad," Logan clipped. "He's wild. So wild he almost ran you and your aunt Cissy over." He bent, pinching Jayden's chin between his fingers and tilting his face up. "Not to mention the babies."

Jayden's face crumpled, his sobs overtaking Logan's words.

"Okay, Logan." Amy removed his hand and stepped between the two. "You've made your point."

She helped Jayden to his feet. Jayden wrapped his arms around her waist and pressed his flushed face against her belly. His tight hold dug into the wound on her side. A fresh rivulet of blood trickled over her skin and dampened her sweater. Amy grimaced, shifting him to a more comfortable position.

"I j-just wa-wanted—"

Jayden's muffled words stopped, his shoulders shaking.

"Shhh," she soothed, smoothing a hand over his blond head and rubbing his back. "It's all right now. Everything turned out okay."

Logan's face darkened. "Amy—"

"He knows he did wrong." She touched her lips to Jayden's shiny hair. "Don't you, Jayden?"

"Y-yes, ma'am," he choked out. He squeezed her waist and buried his face in her sweater again. "I'm s-sorry. I just wanted to..."

His voice turned small and trailed away.

"To help." Amy smiled gently and peered into Logan's angry eyes. "You just wanted to help Thunder be happy. Right?"

"Yes, ma'am," Jayden whispered. He glanced up at Logan and scrubbed the heel of his hand over his cheek. "I just wanted to help, Uncle Logan."

"He's learned his lesson," Amy stressed.

Logan's mouth flattened into a hard line. His dark eyes moved from Jayden's face to Amy's and back again. She held his stare, determined to win this one. Logan shifted restlessly and shoved his hands in his pockets.

"When I give you a rule, Jayden," he said, "I expect you to obey it from now on. Otherwise, I can't trust you."

"Yes, sir," Jayden whispered.

Logan bent, cupped Jayden's head with a broad hand and kissed his forehead. He opened the door and held it, gesturing toward the warmth emanating from inside the house.

"Put him to bed, Amy." Logan glanced at her side and frowned. "Then come to the bathroom and let me change that bandage."

She raised a brow and nudged Jayden. "Your uncle Logan's kind of bossy. I don't think he knows the magic word."

Jayden smiled. He whispered, "It's *please*, Uncle Logan."

Logan's mouth twitched. Those beautiful eyes of his lifted and locked on hers. "Please," he said, voice husky.

Amy's belly warmed. She ducked her head and slipped past him into the house. She was as much a sucker as he was.

Amy led Jayden to his bedroom, helped him and Kayden wash their faces and brush their teeth, then tucked them into bed. Kayden returned her good-night kiss, snuggled into his pillow and watched with interest as Amy sat on the edge of Jayden's mattress, smoothing her fingers through his blond hair.

"What you did today was wrong, Jayden," she said. "No matter how much you think you were doing right."

"Yes, ma'am." Jayden hiccupped. "I won't never do it again."

"Promise?" Amy narrowed her eyes.

"Promise."

"He deserves a butt whoopin'," Kayden proclaimed. "Can I give it to him?"

Amy forced back a smile and cast Kayden a stern look. He shrugged and turned over to face the wall, dragging the covers up over his shoulder.

"Are you gonna give me a spanking, Aunt Amy?" Jayden asked. His blue eyes widened, engulfing his face.

She smiled and ran a finger over his forehead, tucking back a blond curl. "No. I think you've learned your lesson, don't you?"

He nodded, expression earnest.

"Okay." Amy stood. "I want you both to close your eyes and go to sleep. That way you'll be well rested and ready to deliver a good apology to Uncle Dominic and Aunt Cissy in the morning."

She crossed the room and flicked off the light, tugging on the doorknob as she stepped into the hallway.

"Aunt Amy?" Kayden poked his chin above the covers. "Can you leave the door cracked so we can hear when Aunt Cissy gets home?"

"Of course," she whispered. "Now, close your eyes and go to sleep."

"Yes, ma'am," they said in unison.

Amy released the doorknob, allowing a slant of light to pierce the dark quiet of the room. She took a few steps down the hall but paused when the rustling of bedsheets sounded.

"I'm glad we got two aunts now." Jayden's hushed voice carried into the hallway. "They're better than a mama any day."

A bed creaked.

"Yep. Aunt Amy's cool," Kayden said. "But you're lucky she didn't give you a butt whoopin'. A mama woulda burned your tail up."

Jayden sighed. "Yeah, pro'ly. We'd both have us a thousand butt whoopins by now."

It was silent for a moment.

"Maybe," Kayden whispered. "But we ain't got one yet."

A burst of muffled giggles rang out. Amy grinned, covering her mouth to silence her laughter and cradling her side at the sharp sting running through the cut. She leaned against the wall and closed her eyes.

The moment was so familiar. Full of laughter coming from little ones tucked in their beds. She'd imagined it a million times when she'd been pregnant with Sara. And, had her luck been as good back then as it had been for Cissy earlier, the laughter would be coming from her children. Hers and Logan's. Safe in their beds. Loved and protected.

She'd been so sure back then that she could've made Logan happy. Could've won him over, earning a loving husband and strong family. But she'd gone about it the wrong way and ended up losing everything.

Amy sighed. All that was in the past. It was just a teenage crush she'd worked hard to overcome. She'd gotten over her unrealistic hero worship of Logan. She wasn't that desperate girl begging for his attention any more. She was moving on.

She made her way to their old bedroom, shutting the door quietly behind her. It was exactly as she remembered. The small fireplace on the far wall was still charming and the deep polish of the cherry furniture shone as bright as ever. Her purse sat on the dresser and her overnight bags were lined up against the wall by the wide, king-sized bed.

Amy rubbed her hands over her arms and crossed to the dresser. She rifled through the contents of her purse, pulling out the crumpled divorce agreement and smoothing the creases.

The bathroom door opened and Logan exited, his bare feet whispering over the carpet as he crossed the room. He reached out, plucked the papers from her and flicked them down on the dresser.

"Come on." His strong hand wrapped gently around her elbow, tugging her to the bathroom.

He'd discarded his shirt and the thick muscles of his bare back tightened with each of his movements. Amy swallowed hard. It was a physical reaction. Nothing more. She tried to convince herself she'd have the same response to any other well-built man she came across.

Logan stopped in front of the sink. He sifted through the medicine cabinet, retrieving alcohol wipes, fresh gauze and tape.

Amy flicked her eyes around the bathroom, trying to focus on anything other than the broad expanse of his chest. A sprinkling of dark hair arrowed down his abs toward unsnapped jeans hanging low on his lean hips.

Logan's tanned hands gathered the hem of her sweater.

"I can do this myself," she said, stilling his thick wrists.

"You can't reach it properly."

"Yes, I can. Clear out and I'll take care of it."

"Amy, it's been a hell of a day. Just let me do this and let's get some decent sleep. In a bed, this time." He raised a brow and flashed a crooked grin. "Please."

Her body sagged, his gentle expression melting her defenses. She raised her arms, squeezing her eyes shut as he lifted the sweater over her head and dropped it to the tiled floor.

"I swear, Amy, you're about as hardheaded as those boys…"

She glanced up. His eyes clung to the ring dangling from her necklace and the strong column of his throat moved on a hard swallow.

Her face flamed. She should've taken it off long ago. Her hand shot to her chest, pressing over the metal. The stone cut into her palm.

"Logan—"

"Lean to the side," he said, voice hoarse and strained.

She sighed and twisted to the side.

His broad hands moved slowly against her skin, peeling off the old bandage and sweeping an alcohol wipe across the wound. Amy winced at the sting. Logan lowered his dark head, blowing gently across the cut until she relaxed.

"There," he whispered, pressing the last bit of tape over the gauze and a kiss to her rib cage.

Amy tucked her chin to her chest, cheeks burning under his scrutiny. "Thanks."

Logan rose, running his hands along her sides. The heat from his sculpted abs and wide chest pulsed against her front. His fingers caressed her hips and tugged her closer.

She tensed her stomach, trying to ignore the warm flutters spreading beneath her skin, waiting for the moment to pass. It was a physical reaction, nothing more.

Logan's calloused fingers slipped underneath the ring and lifted it.

"You still wear it," he murmured.

Amy blinked, eyes tracing the gray grout outlining each of the square tiles on the floor.

"For how long?" he asked, tugging the ring. "Since you left?"

She looked up and nodded.

Logan's brow creased. His dark eyes clung to hers. He hesitated, his mouth opening and closing, voice finally emerging in a choked rasp.

"There've been no other men?"

Amy cringed. She wished she could lie to him one more time. Tell him he no longer mattered to her. That what she'd felt for him had never been real. That she'd forgotten him long ago and fallen for another man along the way.

That would be enough for him to give in, give up on their marriage and let this go. Then she could move further into her new life. Away from her past sins and embarrassments.

Only, that's how they'd ended up here to begin with. Her past lie still stood between them, casting a shadow and undermining his faith in her. She'd forced his hand back then and didn't deserve his trust now.

Still, she wanted it. Even if she wasn't worthy of it. Amy recoiled, feeling as small as Jayden. Wanting to do so much good and failing in every respect.

Logan's face flushed, the redness flooding his lean cheeks and racing down his broad chest. The muscles in his abs rippled on an indrawn breath.

"Amy?"

A soft tremor shook his voice, highlighting the dark uncertainty in his eyes and deepening the lines of pain on his face.

Amy sighed, shoulders sagging. It was just as Cissy had said. There was never any winning with a Slade man. Especially Logan. He wouldn't let this go. And she couldn't lie to him again. Or to herself. No matter how much she wished she could. Like Jayden, she'd learned her lesson.

She closed her eyes, curled her fingers into his tousled hair and tugged him close. His forehead was warm against hers and she smoothed her palms down to cup his jaw, the only fair words there were leaving her. Honest ones.

"There *are* no other men, Logan. Not like you. They don't exist."

A strangled groan rumbled in his throat, vibrating against her lips as his mouth plundered hers. She wrapped her arms around his broad shoulders, bending beneath his tender advance.

She should stop him. Should finish this before it started. But the hard heat of his chest and the rough rasp of his stubble-lined cheek against her skin renewed old longings.

The longing to be seen by him. To be desired by him. To be loved by him.

His tongue parted her lips and his fingers pressed through the fall of her hair to knead the back of her neck. His hands slid down her back to cradle her bottom, lifting her and wrapping her legs around his waist.

Her chest swelled and a lick of heat curled low in her belly. His masculine scent and gentle touch enveloped her, permeating her senses and settling back into their rightful place in her heart. And, God help her, she'd had no idea how empty she'd been.

She hugged him closer as he carried her into the bedroom and tossed them both onto the bed, the plush bedding cushioning her back and his hard length spanning her front. The moist warmth of his mouth left hers to travel across her skin, lingering on her breasts, thighs and everywhere in between, dispensing with their clothes along the way.

Gasping, she nuzzled the hard curve of his bicep as he settled between her thighs. He pressed deep and a soft cry escaped her, body adjusting, remembering.

He murmured warm words of apology against her lips, then continued with extreme care, body rigid and quaking. She tucked her heels around his thick thighs and pressed her nails into his muscular buttocks, urging him on.

"I won't break," she whispered, kissing his temple. "Let go. Make love to me."

He sucked in a strong breath and moved with greater strength and purpose, limbs steadying. Her hand moved of its own accord, pressing tight to his chest, absorbing the comforting pound of his heart and taking everything he would give.

"Make love to me," she repeated. "Make love to me."

The phrase fell from her lips with each of their movements, hovering on the air between them. She didn't know when the mantra changed. Didn't notice when the words rearranged or when some dropped away.

She only realized it after they both found release. When he rolled to his back, arms wrapped tight around her and she followed. When she replaced her hand at his chest with her wet cheek. Just as she had the first time they'd been together.

The plea lingered on her tongue, breaking the silence, just as it had all those years ago. It echoed around them and within her, mingling with the thundering beat of his heart and the searing heat sweeping over her skin.

"Love me. Love me."

And she wanted him more than she ever had before.

"I'M SORRY."

Logan grimaced. He knew it was the wrong time to tell her. Could feel it in the stiffening of Amy's spine beneath his fingertips and the slow lift of her face from his chest. But he needed to say it. Needed to pry it from his gut and put it down. So they'd at least have a fighting chance.

"For everything," he said. "All the way back to the very start."

Amy rose to her elbows and faced him. Her brow creased, her lush mouth parting on shallow breaths. The light sheen of sweat on her flushed cheeks glistened in the lamplight.

His body tightened. He dropped his gaze, studying the raven tangles of her hair pooling against the white blanket beneath them.

"I remember the exact day things changed between us." He dug deep for the right words. The ones he'd arranged so carefully. "I was twenty. Had finished a good day's work and took off on my own. Rode hard. Decided to stop off by the creek to let the horse take a breather. I was half asleep propped up against that old oak tree when I heard you coming." His mouth curved, a small smile fighting its way out despite his unease. "Your feet snapped a twig or two and I figured you were sneaking up on me. Pulling a prank like you always did. So I kept my eyes shut and played along."

Amy's flush deepened. "Logan—"

"But that's not what you wanted." His mouth tightened. "You kissed me, instead." He tapped a fingertip to his lips, warmth spreading from the spot and heating his face. "Right here."

She squirmed against him and he curled his hand over the curve of her hip, stilling her.

"I was just to practice on, you said. That some guy had caught your eye and you wanted to be prepared." He laughed, the sound grating over his ears. "You turned beet-red. Just like now."

Amy winced and looked down. The long sweep of her hair cascaded over her shoulders, hiding her face.

"I was still a kid," she whispered.

"You were sixteen. Had that beautiful hair and flirty grin. And I knew you were lying." He reached out, brushing her hair back and rubbing the strands between his fingers. "It caught me by surprise. I'd only ever thought of you as a friend and was under the impression you felt the same way about me." His gut churned. "I remember wishing you'd shift that attention to Dom or some other boy closer to your age. Because all I could think was…if I don't put a stop to this, I'm not just gonna lose my best friend, I'm gonna break this girl's heart."

She glanced up, gorgeous green eyes welling.

"And, damn me to hell, Amy," he choked, "that's exactly what I did."

She shook her head and placed her palm to his jaw. "You tried to let me down easy. I know it had to be awkward for you, and you did your best to set me straight over the years."

"My best wasn't good enough."

"You tried. That's the important thing," she said, looking away. "What happened later was my fault. And none of it matters now."

His throat tightened, heart bleeding for her. For the innocent girl she'd been. And the guarded woman she'd become. He lifted his hands, cradling her cheeks and dropping gentle kisses across her face.

He may have made mistakes by eventually giving in to Amy. By not keeping his distance. But when he'd learned of the pregnancy, he'd chosen to marry her despite the fact that she'd deceived him. As her husband, it'd been his job to protect her and he'd failed her. His throat closed. It'd been his job as Sara's father to protect her, too.

Sara.

Logan froze. A wave of nausea swept through him, flooding his mouth. Just their daughter's name was enough to bring the pain back. Enough to remind him of how much they'd lost.

"It doesn't have to all be for nothing, Amy." His voice sounded strange, even to his own ears. "However we got here, this is where we ended up. We still have a chance to build something solid. Something real." He looked up, hating himself as much as he hated the hard glint in her eyes. "You're not still looking for a fairy tale, are you?"

Her mouth tightened. She turned away again, gazing blankly beyond his left shoulder.

"No."

Logan sighed. "We can make this work."

"No. We can't."

Amy pulled against his hold. His hands shot out, tugging her back against him.

"Why not?" He pressed his forehead to hers. "We were best friends once and can be again. That alone will make our marriage strong. We're good together. We proved that earlier with Thunder and just now."

"What just happened was a mistake. One we're not going to repeat."

A mistake. Logan's chest burned. "We're still married."

"Not for much longer." She tossed her hair over her shoulders. "I've been truthful with you this time around,

Logan. You knew exactly what my intentions were coming here."

"I heard you say it. But I can't believe it's what you really want. Raintree is your home. Your family's here." He curved his hand around her jaw, her skin warm under his palm. "I'm here. I want you with me and I want this marriage to work."

She shook her head. "Only because you feel obligated. You didn't want to be married to me. Didn't love me that way—"

"I cared for you." He gathered her against his chest. "I still do. I know that doesn't sound impressive. But love is just a word, Amy. One that people throw around as an excuse for reckless behavior."

Logan's mouth twisted. His mother had used it often enough. She'd said it every time she'd placed her needs before his or Dominic's. Had whispered it when she'd wanted to manipulate Pop into giving in to another one of her selfish demands. And, eventually, had used it as an excuse to abandon her family for a richer man, shrugging off all responsibility for her actions.

Amy had used it, too. She'd said it to him over and over again after getting pregnant. As though that justified her deceiving him and trapping him into marriage.

He shook his head. "It's just a word. A fantasy. The friendship we had was strong. It was real and my loyalty is, too. We're a good team. Always have been."

Her brow creased, eyes roving over his face, dull and heavy. "As good as Dom and Cissy?"

He clutched her hard and nudged a thigh between hers. "Better. We have history."

A scornful laugh burst from her lips. "Bad history."

"I remember the good. The rest can be forgiven."

"And have you? Forgiven?" Her lips trembled. "And forgotten?"

He stiffened. He wished he could tell her what she wanted to hear. Ease her mind and put the light back in her eyes. But he couldn't.

"I'm trying, Amy. We'll try together. Take things slow. Work at forgiving and trusting each other again."

The forgetting he wasn't so sure about.

Her breasts lifted against him on an inhale. "Let's just be for now. I'm tired."

She sounded it. The husky note in her tone and heaviness in her limbs proved it.

Logan moved to his back, holding her close and trailing his fingers in wide circles over the smooth skin of her back.

"Then go to sleep," he said. "I'll be here when you wake up."

And he would be. Every day. He could get things right this time. Remind her how good they could be together and prove their marriage wasn't a mistake. That their daughter hadn't been a mistake. He owed it to Amy and they both owed it to Sara.

He shifted, bundling Amy against him and sliding beneath the covers. She drifted off before he tucked the sheet around her, hand resting over his heart and quiet breath whispering across his chest.

Logan tried to follow. Closed his eyes and tried to dream. But he couldn't silence his thoughts. Could only continue wondering silently how Amy could be right in his arms but still feel a million miles away.

Chapter Seven

"Over this way, Amy."

Logan tapped the brim of his Stetson lower on his brow and leaned over the fence rail. Amy stood in the center of the round pen edging around Thunder's frantic bucks. Just as she'd been doing every day for the past three weeks with no progress to show for it.

Amy passed one palm after the other farther up the lead rope, stepping slowly across the ground toward Thunder. Logan tensed.

"Something's off." Dominic shifted at his side and propped a boot on a low fence rung.

"I know," Traci said. She grabbed Dominic's shoulder and pulled, leveraging herself up to straddle the fence. "Thunder gets more aggressive every day."

Logan sighed. He hated to admit it but it was the truth.

Every morning for the past few days, he'd woken before dawn to find Amy gone. By the time he yanked on clothes and made it outside, she'd had Thunder in the round pen, attempting to run ground work.

Attempting was the only word for it. She'd been at it for hours today, just like all the others, with no change in the stallion. Thunder ducked his head and attacked on several occasions, causing Amy to scale the fence more than usual. And every time Logan or Dominic tried to help, Thunder became more violent and left Amy even more discouraged. It seemed as though whatever ground she'd gained with Thunder, she'd lost it just as fast.

Logan grimaced and scraped his boot over the ground. Amy hadn't been herself since he'd brought her home but she'd definitely been more out of sorts lately. The only explanation for it was their sexual encounter three weeks earlier.

He didn't blame Amy for backing away. He blamed himself. With everything that had happened between them, he should've been more controlled. Shouldn't have let the chaos of that day and one shared moment of success coax his guard down.

It seemed his body was as intent on betraying him as much now as it had before. But despite that, he couldn't bring himself to regret making love to her. He'd missed her over the years and it'd felt good to comfort her. To be comforted. To hold her again.

But he felt as removed from Amy now as he would if she were already in Michigan. And only a couple of weeks remained before she left.

Logan balled his fists. *Time.* He'd never been on good terms with it. The earth could crack under his feet and the fool sun would still rise. But as soon as a moment of peace arrived, night would swallow it whole. Time kept ticking no matter what occurred.

"There he goes again." Dominic smacked his palm on the fence, rattling it under Logan's elbows as Thunder lunged and missed Amy by inches. "I'm worried she's gonna get hurt. He's starting to wear her down."

"She's being careful," Logan murmured.

Hell if he knew who he was trying to reassure. Dominic? Or himself?

"Angle over this way, Amy." Logan waved a hand, keeping his tone calm. "I can boost you over if he charges again."

Dominic sighed. "I know she doesn't want to hear it but have you talked to her? Asked her to ease off a bit? Take a break?"

"I've tried," Logan said. "But she's adamant she can bring Thunder around. Keeps fantasizing that he can be saved."

"It's not a fantasy, Logan. There's always a chance. But she needs to take a step back. Rest and regroup. Let us take over for a while."

"That won't help," Logan said. "Thunder trusts us less than he does her. And no amount of time is going to change the final outcome."

"So, that's your solution?" Dominic cocked an eyebrow. "Just give up? She can handle him, Logan. More than handle him if she gets her bearings again." He jerked his chin at the enclosure. "She's gentled more horses in that pen than I can count."

"This is different."

"How? There's a horse and a round pen. Same as before."

"It's not the same—"

"Shhhh."

Logan jerked his head back around to find Amy scowling in their direction. Thunder, rattled by her hiss, snaked his head and charged. Logan shot over the top rail, catching Amy as she jumped out of Thunder's path and assisting her over the fence.

She pushed his hands away, tossed her hair back

and frowned. "I can handle myself. Could've handled Thunder, too, if the two of you hadn't been running your loud mouths."

Dominic cast a halfhearted smile at Amy. "We know you can, Ames." His face softened. "We're just worried about you. You've had a lot of close calls with Thunder lately and we don't want you getting hurt. If anyone can help Thunder, you can. But you can't be effective in that pen if you run yourself into the ground. You haven't been yourself for a while and Thunder's picking up on it."

Amy rubbed her forehead. "I know that. I'm just frustrated."

She glanced behind her, shoulders sagging. Logan followed her gaze to the far side of the enclosure where Thunder kicked and stomped.

"I'm doing the same things I've always done," she whispered. "I don't know why he won't respond."

Logan studied her weary expression and cringed. Dominic was right. She needed some space. Some time to relax.

Logan plucked a piece of dead grass from her sleeve then rubbed his hands up and down her arms. "Well, forcing it isn't going to help you or Thunder. You need to take a break and clear your head."

Squeals broke out behind them. Jayden sprinted across the field at high speed, his brother chasing close on his heels. They kicked up clouds of dust that hovered in sunlit particles behind them and drew to an abrupt halt at the fence.

"I won." Jayden doubled over, air rasping between his lips.

"Only 'cuz you cheated." Kayden shoved his brother

then swaggered over to Amy. He propped his hands on his hips and squinted at Thunder thrashing in the pen. "You ain't whipped that horse, yet, Aunt Amy?"

"She's not gonna whip anything," Jayden huffed. "She don't give spankings." He skipped over and tipped his head back to look up at Amy. "Ain't that right?"

Amy laughed and hugged the boys to her legs. Her entire demeanor changed. The rigid tension in her body released and the tight lines on her brow eased.

Logan's chest swelled. This was Amy. As she had been. Bright and energetic. Warm and inviting. The way she was before they'd lost so much.

"Oh, you know what I mean," Kayden drawled, squinting up at Amy. "You could whoop any horse into shape. Uncle Dominic said so."

Amy glanced at Dominic. "That's nice of him to say. But I don't think Thunder likes me messing with him. I think he'd prefer to run me over."

"You want me to help you?" Kayden puffed his chest out. "I won't let no horse come after you."

Amy smiled. "Thanks for the offer, Kayden." She bent and kissed his cheek. "But I wouldn't want to risk you getting hurt."

Kayden shrugged, his features firming. "Okay. But if Thunder shows his butt, you tell me and I'll whoop him for ya so you won't have to."

"Me, too," Jayden said, sharing a conspiratorial look with Kayden. "We'll both give him a butt whoopin'."

The boys dissolved into a fit of giggles, wrapping around Amy's legs and snorting.

"Lord have mercy," Traci muttered, grinning. "Any horse would take off as soon as they saw the two of you coming."

"Uh-uh," Kayden jeered. "Besides, I know what Aunt Amy's doing wrong."

Kayden darted between Dominic's legs and climbed onto the fence rail next to Traci.

He rubbed a grubby hand over his face, leaving a streak of dirt on his cheek. "She ain't spitting."

Traci issued a sound of disgust. "What does that have to do with anything, squirt?"

"Everything." Kayden lifted his chin. "Mr. Jed said if something's broke on a ranch, it just needs some spit-shine and elbow grease." He smiled, teeth gleaming. "She needs to spit on him."

Dominic laughed and ruffled Kayden's hair. "I think you're spending entirely too much time with Mr. Jed. Why don't you give the hands a break and let 'em work without you underfoot today."

Kayden's nose wrinkled. "Mr. Jed ain't no hand. He said he's a bone-a-fine cowboy. Like you and Uncle Logan."

"That's *bona fide*." Traci said, lips twitching.

"Yeah, that's what I said." Kayden pursed his lips in affront then grinned. "Anyways, Mr. Jed likes us help-ing him. He gives us good jobs, and he pays us."

Logan smiled. Grumpy Jed probably came up with something all right. The boys had started trailing Jed the second they were released from school for Christ-mas break yesterday and hadn't stopped since.

"What kind of job did he give you today?" Amy asked, smoothing a palm over Jayden's back.

"He gave us a dollar to sit by the fence he painted and make sure it dried." Kayden shrugged. "But that got boring so we left. Then we couldn't find him."

Amy laughed. "Well, that's his loss."

Jayden tugged at Amy's wrist. "Are you a bone-a-fine cowgirl, Aunt Amy?"

She smiled down at him. "I don't know. Depends on who you ask. Everyone has their idea of one. Do you think I'm one?"

"Yep." Jayden grinned. "That's how come you can whoop any horse into shape."

"Yeah and Uncle Dominic said you can beat anyone on a horse," Kayden said, flashing a sly look at Logan. "Said you used to beat Uncle Logan every time y'all raced."

Logan narrowed his eyes at Kayden. "Not every time. I won on occasion."

"Sometimes, but not often," Amy said, laughing.

Jayden's eyes widened with excitement. "Are you gonna race Uncle Logan today?"

Amy's laugh tapered off and she glanced back at the round pen. "I don't have time for a race. I need to work with Thunder some more."

The shadows returned to her eyes and her expression fell.

Logan shook his head. "Not a good idea. You've been at it long enough."

"But—"

"No buts. Jayden has a good point. You need a break and so does Thunder. I think a ride is a great idea." Logan pulled at Jayden's belt loop, pausing to unwind the boy's arms from around Amy's legs with a chuckle. "Let your aunt Amy go, buddy. She's already taken."

Jayden frowned. "Who's takin' her somewhere?"

Logan returned Amy's grin. "Me."

Kayden sprang down from the fence, ran over and

stood beside his brother. Both boys put their hands on their hips and narrowed their eyes up at Logan.

"Where you takin' her?" Kayden asked.

"For a ride on a horse," Logan said.

"How far?"

"Far."

The boys pondered that, their wide blue eyes moving from him to rest on Amy.

"You wanna go with him?" Kayden asked.

Amy smiled and nodded.

Jayden huffed, jutting his chin out at Logan. "You better bring her back."

"I will," Logan murmured, body tightening at the warmth in Amy's green eyes. Her throat moved on a hard swallow and she looked away. "I promise."

"Hey." Kayden darted off and yanked at Dominic's jeans. "Is it time for the bonfire yet?"

Logan grinned at the excitement gleaming in Amy's eyes. Every year, Raintree kicked off the week of Christmas with a special celebration for family and guests. The night consisted of tasty treats, games for the kids, lighting the large cypress tree behind the main house, and a big bonfire.

Every child on the ranch received an ornament, painted their name on it and hung it on the tree. Then, the bonfire would be lit to make sure Santa had a clear view of all the names. Pop used to say the bonfire was Raintree's way of getting the Nice list to Santa.

Logan shook his head. He'd never been conned into believing it. But as children, Dominic and Amy had. The flames had burned so bright and high they had believed the message reached all the way to heaven.

Logan remembered how excited Amy had always

gotten over the annual Christmas bonfire as a kid and her joy for it had never diminished. It'd been years since she'd been home for one.

"Not yet," Dominic said. "Needs to be good and dark first, then Uncle Logan will get it lit."

"Can we light the bonfire, Uncle Logan?" Kayden asked.

Logan suppressed the shudder sweeping through him. It wouldn't take the twins more than ten seconds with a match to send Raintree up in flames.

"No," he said. "I think it's best to leave that to the grown-ups."

Dominic winked and nudged Kayden's chin with a knuckle. "Uncle Logan lights it every year. We don't want to break tradition, do we?"

Kayden frowned but shook his head.

"How 'bout we go in for some hot chocolate?" Dominic suggested. "Traci and I will get you fixed up with some marshmallows. After that, we can help Mr. Jed and the rest of the hands get the wood stacked for the bonfire."

The boys squealed at that. Jayden ran over and tugged at Traci's arm.

"Can I get the big marshmallows this time? I don't like the small ones."

Traci hopped down off the fence and took Jayden's hand in hers. "They both taste the same, Jayden."

"No, they don't."

"If Jayden gets the big ones then so do I," Kayden grumped.

"Rein it in, Kayden, or you won't get any marshmallows." Dominic scooped Kayden up and settled him atop his shoulders, holding his hands as he started walking across the field.

Jayden scampered after his brother and Dominic, pulling Traci behind him and hollering over his shoulder, "You better bring Aunt Amy back, Uncle Logan. You promised."

"Keep it quiet when we get inside, boys," Dominic said. "Your aunt Cissy's probably still napping."

Their *Yes, sirs* faded into the distance.

"You don't want to ride, Dom?" Amy called.

Dominic twisted, tossing a dimpled grin over his shoulder. "Nah, I've had my share of riding. I want to check on Cissy."

The group ambled off toward the main house.

"He's changed." Amy stared after Dominic as he made his way across the field.

"Yeah," Logan said. "Took a while, but he finally decided to settle down. Cissy and the boys had a lot to do with that."

She glanced at him. "Does he still compete at rodeos?"

"No." Logan shook his head. "The last time he rode a bull was over a year ago. He talks about starting up that bull-riding clinic but he's been preoccupied with preparing for the babies lately. When it comes to Cissy, those bulls don't stand a chance with Dom."

Amy looked back at Dominic making his way up the wide, front porch steps, Kayden on his shoulders and Jayden at his side. "He left the circuit for her?"

Her lips barely moved over the quiet words. Logan's chest tightened at the air of yearning that surrounded her. That familiar wistfulness was in the stillness of her body and the features of her face. It was an air that had clung to her over the years. One he'd first seen shining in her eyes when she'd kissed him by that oak tree all those years ago.

"She's his wife." Logan moved close, touching her jaw and bringing her face back to his. "A man stays with his family. That's the way it should be."

Her eyes dropped and her resigned half smile hit him hard in the gut.

Heaven help him, he missed her. Missed *them*. He wanted to rebuild their friendship and remind her of who she used to be before her spirit was broken. Return that sweet look of wistfulness to her face and feel it warm his skin when she looked at him.

You better bring her back.

Logan smiled. Jayden was on to something, all right. And that was exactly what he was gonna do. "Now, let's go for that ride."

AMY TILTED HER head back and strained to catch the faint touch of warmth from the setting sun. The late afternoon air had grown colder over the course of her ride with Logan across Raintree's grounds.

A wave of dizziness swept over her, causing her weight to shift off-center in the saddle. She grabbed the saddle horn and straightened. Lightning huffed beneath her and shook his head. His white mane tossed about, settling in disarray over her fingers.

Amy made herself heavy, re-centered her balance and weighed her seat down. She blinked rapidly, clearing the dancing spots from her vision and refocused on the horizon.

It was nothing new. For the past week, she'd had the same type of spell almost every day and had felt...*off*.

It had to be stress. She'd had her fair share of it since she returned home, and working with Thunder only exacerbated her emotional state.

Amy relaxed as the world centered again. She delivered gentle pats to Lightning's neck. He nickered and slowed his steps, the day's dying light caressing his pale mane in a glow of pink.

It'd be dark soon and would only get colder. There was so much work that still needed to be done with Thunder. It was past time to turn back.

"It's still Saturday, yeah?"

Logan's deep tenor disrupted her thoughts. He cut her a sidelong glance, dark eyes narrowing beneath the brim of his tan Stetson. His broad hands pulled back on his reins to fall into step beside her.

She frowned and nodded. "Why?"

He shrugged, broad shoulders stretching his blue shirt, and grinned. "Just wondering why you're taking a Sunday stroll."

Amy warmed at his sly look. She dropped her gaze, only to find it hovering over the tight denim covering his muscular thigh.

"I'm enjoying a relaxing ride," she said. "Taking a break like you suggested."

"At this rate, it'll take two weeks to cross the grounds. Feels like we've been trudging along at this pace for days already." He jerked his chin toward Lightning. "He's restless."

As if on cue, Lightning tossed his head and stomped.

Amy's mouth tightened. "No, he's not."

"Yeah. He is."

She raised a brow at his deliberate tone. "So what are you suggesting?"

His grin widened. "A harmless competition between friends."

"I take it you want to race."

"Isn't that how our rides always used to turn out?"

Amy smirked. "Pretty much. And, if memory serves, Kayden was correct in saying I always won."

"Not always."

"Yeah. I did."

Logan laughed, the deep, sexy rumble surrounding her and tingling on her skin. "Then you shouldn't have a problem defending your title."

Amy hesitated, gaze lingering over the warm depths of his eyes and teasing grin. It was a bad idea. She should be back at the round pen, at least trying to run Thunder through the paces.

She'd promised to bring the stallion back to his old self and hadn't made a lick of progress. Thunder was the last hurdle she had to overcome before leaving. One that would enable her to pack her bags and walk away to a fresh start, leaving the empty ache in her chest behind.

Only, it was becoming harder to believe she could ever banish it altogether. The four-year absence from Raintree had left her longing for home. These last few weeks had reminded her how much she missed it. And most—*or worst*—of all, making love with Logan had reminded her of exactly how much she missed *him*.

They'd continued to sleep beside each other in the same bed. Most nights, she'd fallen asleep on her side, carefully keeping her distance. But each morning, she'd woken up in Logan's arms, then slipped away quickly while he slept. She'd never been able to give Logan her body without handing over her heart. Still couldn't. And

Logan's heart was something he'd never been willing to share with her.

Amy sighed. Could what Logan offered be enough? Maybe he was right. Maybe she was too hung up on a fantasy. The kind that didn't exist. Maybe what he offered was as real as love could get.

"You're thinking too much." Logan moved his mount closer and placed his big palm on her thigh.

Amy's leg tensed. His tender caress penetrated her jeans, slipped beneath her skin and danced in her blood. It rushed higher and filled her chest with a sweet heaviness. The same sweet welling of heat that bloomed when Logan held her, his heart beating beneath her cheek.

Amy closed her eyes and squeezed the saddle horn tighter. She wished that feeling could last. Wished she could carry it with her, possess it forever and never feel alone.

"Just once," she whispered, clarifying at his confused look. "We'll race one time."

That would be enough. Then she could set this longing down and move on. Let Raintree go. And leave Logan, along with the girl she used to be, behind.

She straightened, tossing her hair over her shoulder and re-centering her seat. "How about we up the stakes, though? You win, I muck the stalls. I win, the hat's mine?"

Logan's mouth twisted, his tone hesitant. "Don't know about that. A man should never be parted from his hat." He tapped the brim with his finger. "And this is a damned good one."

She laughed. "So, you know you're gonna lose."

He knuckled the Stetson up an inch, narrowing his eyes and smiling. "Didn't say that, babe."

Amy's heart tripped in her chest. Logan's flirtatious gaze seared over her, heating her skin. How many times had she wished for that look from him over the years? And to get it now…

A man stays with his family.

How she still wanted that. Wanted Logan at her side every day. His child in her arms.

His child. Amy froze. Dizzy spells for a week. Feeling *off.* Her hand touched the flat plane of her belly. *How long had it been since…?*

She'd arrived home on Thanksgiving Day and she and Logan had made love the night after. Her mind scrambled to count the days, which quickly added up to weeks. *Three weeks.* Almost three weeks to the day since they'd—

No. Her shoulders slumped, a heavy weight settling over her. There was no need to worry on that account. There was next to no chance of it. What had the doctors said after she'd lost Sara? Her chances of conceiving were—*greatly diminished. Highly improbable.* And, in the event of a successful conception, pregnancy was… *inadvisable.*

Amy swiped the back of her hand over her forehead, whisking away cold beads of sweat. *Placental abruption. Stillborn. Hemorrhaging. Scarring.* Cold clinical terms for something so horrifying.

No. It was highly unlikely. It had taken several times for her to get pregnant before. They'd only been together the one time and she'd been late more than once over the years. But never this late.

Amy's stomach churned, her palms growing sweaty. She didn't know which emotion railed at her more. The paralyzing fear of possibly being pregnant. Or the over-whelming pain of never being able to conceive.

A frigid wind swept through, masking the sun's fading warmth. A streak of adrenaline shot through her veins and shook her limbs, the urge to bolt hitting her hard.

The endless acres before her beckoned, the dormant ground unobstructed and ripe for the taking. Amy tightened her legs around Lightning. He jerked his head, drawing to a reluctant halt.

Lightning wanted to run. So did she. More than anything.

"Whatcha say, handsome?" Amy asked, combing her trembling fingers through Lightning's coarse mane and striving for a calm tone. "Want to show him up?"

Amy lowered her torso, lightened her seat and clutched the reins. The command from years ago bloomed in her chest, rose to tickle her tongue and escaped on a panicked whisper.

"Fly, boy."

Lightning heaved forward, hooves pounding over the ground, spraying up dead grass and clumps of mud. Amy moved with him, staying steady and centered. The stallion's powerful lunges stirred excitement in her veins. It buzzed in her blood, strengthening her posture and dancing on the surface of her skin.

Each foot of distance brought back her balance and soothed her senses, reminding her of how she used to feel. Brave. Carefree. *Alive.*

She hooked the reins around the saddle horn and rose up, firming her grip with her thighs and stretching her arms out to catch the rush of wind with her palms. Cold air licked through her hair, teasing her neck and slipping beneath the billowed back of her shirt.

The throbbing gallop of Logan's stallion sounded at her side. Amy glanced to her left. Logan leaned forward, his muscular thighs hugging his horse's middle, his powerful build steady, keeping pace with her.

He smiled. "That all you got, babe?"

Amy laughed, a rebellious energy she hadn't felt in years firing through her body. The wind roared by her ears, her heart pounded and a sweet sense of freedom overcame her. She renewed her hold on the reins and gave Lightning permission to charge faster. They regained the lead, sprinting a foot ahead and swallowing up the spacious fields before them. Logan remained hot on their heels.

Lightning stretched his legs in long, galloping leaps following a familiar path until they crossed the edge of the open field. He slowed to a walk as they came to a cluster of trees lining a rushing creek and carefully maneuvered between them until they reached the bank.

"Good boy," she crooned.

Amy kissed Lightning's sweaty neck, drew him to a halt and glanced over her shoulder. Logan stroked his horse's neck and eased up beside her. She examined his devilish expression, narrowing her eyes on the sexy curve of his smile.

"You held back and let me win."

Logan chuckled. "Are you implying you couldn't have outrun me otherwise?"

"No. Just making an observation."

"So, considering that, I get to keep my hat."

"I don't know," she said. "I'll have to think about it."

She swung her leg over Lightning's back and hopped

down, watching as the stallion walked to the creek and began to drink. Logan followed suit and led his horse over to join Lightning.

Amy turned, eyeing the scattering of trees and noting one in particular. She sighed as she surveyed the solid strength of the oak tree. Its impressive shape and towering height was familiar and stirred an ache in her chest.

She winced, absorbing the rush of embarrassment. It was the same tree Logan had leaned against when she'd first kissed him. It had taken every drop of bravery she'd had to touch her lips to his all those years ago. To risk so much for what she knew would be so small a reward.

She'd loved Logan just as strongly then as she loved him now. There was no need to fight it or run from it. It just was. She had to accept it as something she could never change or leave behind.

Amy walked over and leaned against the oak's trunk. She closed her eyes and absorbed the whispering rush of water from the creek and the rough bark at her back, allowing herself to imagine, just for a moment, how different things might have been if she hadn't lost Sara. If she hadn't pushed Logan so hard. If she'd given him a chance to love her back.

She felt fabric sweep past her shoulders and a strong heat drew near to her chest. She opened her eyes to find Logan leaning close, his dark eyes on her mouth and his muscular arms braced against the trunk on both sides of her.

Her belly fluttered as his lips parted, his head dipping.

"Wanna give it another try?" He tapped his mouth with the blunt tip of his finger.

Amy shook her head, heat racing up her neck. She pressed her palms tight to the tree behind her, digging her fingers into the uneven crannies of the bark.

Logan's gaze left her mouth and traveled over her face. His lips tipped up at the corners.

"Come on, babe," he whispered, taking one of her hands in his and holding it to his chest. "Try me."

She pressed her lips together, stilling as his eyes darkened and returned to her mouth. The heavy throb of his heart beat against her palm and coursed down to her wrist, coaxing her pulse to join its rhythm.

"Let's make a better memory," he urged. "One we can enjoy remembering."

God help her, she wanted that. Amy sighed, closing her eyes and touching her mouth to the rough stubble on his cheek. She nuzzled her nose against his skin and breathed him in, savoring his masculine scent. He pressed close and slipped his fingers underneath the ring hanging from her neck.

"Friend, lover, husband…" His husky voice tickled her ear, sending thrills over her skin. "Call it whatever you want." He nudged a leg between hers and lifted his head. "I'm yours, Amy."

Her palms tingled. She wanted nothing more than to hold on to him. To find comfort in his strength.

She slipped her fingertips under the brim of his hat, weaving them through the thick waves of his hair, and parted his lips with hers. A low growl throbbed in his throat and he explored her mouth with gentle sweeps of his tongue. His knuckles brushed her cheek, skimming her shoulders and uncurling to secure a grip on her hip.

Heat speared through her and traveled low, making her ache with need. Seeking a distraction, she burrowed her fingers further into his hair and dislodged his hat, swooping up his Stetson and settling it firmly on her own head. It sat a little loose and knocked against his forehead as he kissed her.

His deep chuckle rumbled. He smiled wide against her mouth, his teeth bumping her lips. Amy grinned, savoring the delight in his eyes and cherishing the abandon in his unrestrained laughter.

"That's my favorite one." He drew back, pinching the hat and centering it on her head. "I should've known better than to risk it with you."

Amy's grin slipped. It was a teasing statement. Benign and meaningless. But it managed to cut.

Logan winced. He framed her face with his warm palms and kissed her forehead.

"Hey," he whispered. "This is a better memory, yeah? A good one."

She nodded, closing her eyes as he claimed her mouth with the softest of kisses. He rubbed his hands up and down her arms in brisk movements and smiled.

"It's getting cold. Let's head back for the bonfire so you can show off your trophy." He tapped the Stetson and grinned. "I know you gotta be chomping at the bit to gloat to Dom."

Amy thumped the brim of the hat and beamed, slowing her speech to her best hick drawl. "A girl's gotta lay claim to her bragging rights, sir. Ain't my fault you held back."

"This time." He laughed, turning to amble away toward the horses. "I might not on the next run. So you better hope you remember everything I taught you."

She dragged her palms over her jeans and ducked her head. That was the biggest problem. She couldn't forget. Any of it. The good or the bad. They were impossible to separate.

Logan whistled. Lightning left the creek and trotted toward him.

Logan turned, stretching out his upturned palm. "Come on. Let's head home."

She placed her hand in his, skin heating at his touch, and mounted Lightning. Logan smiled and left to remount his horse.

Amy eyed the wide expanse of land barely visible between the tangle of trees. A strong wind swept across her overheated skin. It rushed through the long strands of her hair, jerking them over her shoulders and in front of her face in wild arcs.

Lightning stomped, his muscled bulk shifting beneath her as he shook his head, ready to take off again. Amy rubbed his neck and murmured soothing words. The wind whipped with greater strength, causing the trees to sway, limbs to dip and the swift current of the creek to intensify. Even the ground trembled with excitement beneath her as Lightning took a few impatient steps.

Amy inhaled, chest rising and shoulders lifting. The moment was so familiar. Raintree as it had been. Alive and exciting.

Logan laughed. "You look all of nineteen again in that hat."

Amy opened her eyes to find him at her side.

He swept a strand of hair over her shoulder and his tone deepened. "Ready?"

She nodded, nudging Lightning and undertaking a relaxed pace across the grounds. The wind continued to push at their backs and the festive Christmas lights draping the fences of Raintree's front yard peeked out from the dark stretch of land before them, guiding their way.

Amy squared her shoulders and pushed Logan's Stetson down firmer on her head. Raintree's call grew louder. It beckoned with each sweep of cold air, twinkle of white lights and creak of their saddles. She glanced at Logan, returning his smile with a more cautious one.

Even now, she could feel the girl she'd been unfurling inside, stretching and waking up. Wanting nothing more than to keep riding straight into the warm embrace of the main house and stay in this beautiful place. Needing so much from it and from Logan. Wanting everything despite the cost.

Amy pressed a trembling palm to her midsection, smoothing it hard over the flat plane of her belly. This dance with Logan was dangerous. He and Raintree belonged to the rebellious girl she used to be. Not the honorable woman she'd grown into. She had to remember that. Because she wasn't sure if there was room inside her for both.

Chapter Eight

Logan pushed away the cup of "eggnog" Jayden held out and smiled politely. He had lived long enough to learn the value of self-preservation, and any concoction the twins offered was suspect.

"No, thanks, buddy."

Logan glanced at the massive cypress tree, glowing with white lights. The annual Christmas tree lighting had become a crowd favorite at Raintree. Guests and locals alike turned out every year to help decorate the tree and huddle around the warmth of the festive bonfire.

The group of guests had dwindled down on account of the late hour and most of them had retired to their rooms for the night. Only family remained, along with a few hands who were finishing off the last of their sweet desserts or beer on hay bales used as makeshift seating. Logan spotted Amy silhouetted in the bonfire's blaze, recognizing the familiar shape of his Stetson atop her head.

He grinned. The only time she'd removed it since their ride several hours ago had been when she'd let Kayden climb onto her shoulders to hang a cloth angel on a high branch of the Cypress tree. And, even then, after lowering Kayden to the ground, she'd scooped the hat up and put it right back on.

"But you ain't had no eggnog yet." Jayden stepped on top of Logan's boots and thrust the cup closer to his face.

Logan frowned and examined the liquid. The flickering light from the bonfire blazing several feet away enabled him to make out the white liquid filling the lower half of the clear mug. It looked safe enough. But the thick, red film floating on top turned his stomach and called for hesitation.

He twisted his lips and glanced at Amy. She had her back to him, sharing a laugh with Cissy, Betty and Traci. At least, she wouldn't witness him being a heel.

"Nah, I think I'll pass." Logan lifted Jayden off the tops of his boots and set him back on the ground.

Dominic and Pop shifted at Logan's side, cocking their heads and leveling disapproving frowns on him. *Well, hell.* He'd get no support from them.

"Come on." Dominic nudged Logan. "Don't want to disappoint the little fellas, do you?"

Logan sighed and surveyed the boys. Jayden and Kayden stood side by side, blinking up at him with wounded blue eyes.

His stomach dropped and he shifted uneasily. Nothing stripped your defenses better than kids.

He rubbed a hand over his brow then reached for the cup. "I'm not that big on eggnog, fellas."

"But it's good." Kayden smiled. "We made it special, Uncle Logan."

That, he believed. The strong scent of spices wrinkled his nose as he lifted it to his mouth. He hesitated, holding the cup to his lips.

"Please try it," Jayden said. "Just one taste?"

Logan's mouth twitched. Whether it was from laughter or distaste of what he was about to put in it, he wasn't sure. But he proceeded, tossing back a healthy swallow of the goop.

A flash of heat engulfed his gums and scorched a path down his throat, choking him. He spewed the last globs of it out of his mouth and doubled over. His eyes watered and tears coursed down his cheeks as he gasped.

"Lord, have mercy, Logan."

Betty approached, her shocked voice barely rising over the gales of laughter from Pop and Dominic. A hand slapped his back, pounding hard, then shook his shoulder.

"Get it all out, son," Pop chuckled.

"What in heaven's name have you done to him?" Betty pressed against his side, clutching a glass of sweet tea and peering into his face. "You okay, Logan?"

He snatched the glass from her hand and tossed it back in one gulp. The cold beverage masked the fire coating his throat, allowing him to catch his breath.

Dominic winked. "He just had a taste of the boys' special brew."

"Oh, Dom." Betty clucked her tongue. "I told you to throw that stuff out."

Logan sucked in a lungful of cold air and glared at Dominic. "You mean to tell me you knew what was in that?"

"Of course he did," Betty said, taking both glasses from Logan's hands. "The boys used up every bit of my cayenne powder making this gunk. They thought it was cinnamon. Heaven knows what else they put in it."

Dominic held up his hands and adopted an innocent expression. "Easy now, big bro. I only knew because I got talked into trying it, too."

Logan choked back a laugh, stretched around Pop and grabbed a handful of Dominic's shirt. "You little shi—"

"Language, boys," Cissy admonished.

The rest of the ladies had arrived. Traci covered her mouth as a fit of giggles overtook her and Amy smiled a mile wide. Cissy, however, shoved between the men and rose to her toes, prying Logan's fist from Dominic's shirt.

"Not in front of the little ones." Cissy smoothed her hands over Dominic's collar and the corner of her mouth kicked up. "Besides, my husband looks especially nice tonight and I'd like to keep him that way."

Dominic tugged her close and whispered in her ear. Cissy's cheeks reddened. She batted at Dominic's chest, disentangling herself from his hold and started for the main house.

"Time to go in and get a bath, boys. It's getting late and you both need your rest."

The twins groaned.

"Aw, come on, Aunt Cissy." Kayden scowled. "Just a little longer. We ain't got no school all week."

"That's, *we don't have any school this week*. And from the sound of those double negatives, I think they should've canceled vacation and kept you in class."

"But—"

"I said, no." Cissy stabbed a finger at the ground and smiled. "Now, do your good-night rounds and get your tails over here."

"Best do what she says, Kayden," Dominic whispered, expression grave. "Santa's watching."

Kayden pouted but delivered his good-night kisses to everyone. Jayden followed suit but after kissing Amy's cheek, he wrapped his arms around her hand and pulled.

"Will you come in, too, Aunt Amy? I want you to tuck me in."

"Yeah," Kayden chimed, grabbing Amy's other free hand. "And will you read that same story you read to us last night? No one else does the voices good as you."

She smiled. "I'd love to."

"You gotta do your good-night kisses before you go in," Kayden said solemnly. "It's Aunt Cissy's rule."

Amy laughed. "Well, we don't want to break any rules, do we?"

She pressed a swift kiss to Dominic and Pop's cheeks then peppered a few more all over the boys. They gurgled with giggles and she laughed harder in response. Logan's chest warmed at the sight. The heat from the fire had painted her cheeks a cherry red, making those gorgeous green eyes shine like emeralds.

He'd heard her laugh on several occasions throughout the evening and each delightful bout of it melted away another lost year between them. It was easy to recall the teenage years she'd spent at his side by the Christmas bonfire, plucking marshmallows from his roasting stick and sneaking sips of his mulled wine.

She caught him staring and blushed even more. "Are you coming in?"

"Soon," he said. "I'm gonna help clean up."

"Come on, Aunt Amy." Kayden shoved at her hip. "Give Uncle Logan his good-night kiss so we can go in."

Logan grinned and arched a brow. Amy hesitated,

glancing down at the boys. Their wide blue eyes moved from her to him and back again.

Amy sighed and stepped closer. She brushed her lips against his cheek, lodging a sweet ache in his belly. Logan curled his hand around her hip, tugging her close and nuzzling her neck.

A small hand shoved between them. Jayden scowled up at him and wrapped his arms tight around Amy's leg.

"You already got your good-night kiss, Uncle Logan."

He laughed. "Guess you're right, buddy."

Amy stepped back and tapped the brim of the Stetson with a fingertip. "Good night, gentlemen."

Amy left with the boys, following the other ladies and laughing on the walk back to the main house. Cissy looked over her shoulder and blew a kiss to Dominic.

"I hate to call it quits early, but…" Dominic rubbed his chest and grinned, dimples denting.

Pop held up a hand and smiled. "Say no more, son. We'll wrap things up out here."

Dominic jogged off, catching up with Cissy and hugging her close as they made their way up the path. Amy trailed behind the couple with the boys, pausing every few steps to point at the sky and answer the boys' questions.

"Amy sure has a way with those boys," Pop murmured. "She looks good with 'em."

Logan stiffened. He turned away to watch the hands laugh and pass around another round of beers. Amy did look great with those boys at her sides. But he couldn't shake the last image he'd had of her holding a child.

Their child. Sara. And the sight had been gut-wrenching.

Pop shifted, his elbow brushing against Logan's. He remained silent for a moment, then cleared his throat.

"It's nice having Raintree full again," Pop said. "It'll be even nicer when Cissy and Dom's girls get here. I hate that Amy might not be here when the babies arrive." He hesitated, rocking back on his heels. "How much longer is she staying?"

"A couple weeks." Logan rasped a palm over the stubble lining his jaw and turned away.

"Don't mean to pry but have you talked with her any more about things?" Pop's gaze heated his skin. "I thought Amy might've changed her mind about leaving after she settled in."

"No." Logan shoved his hands in his pockets. "I'm still working on getting her to stay put."

"You two seem a lot closer now than when she first came home." Pop nodded as if in reassurance. "That girl still loves you. Always has. No amount of time or distance will change that."

"You sure about that?" Logan faced him. "You thought the same thing about Mom and we all know how that turned out."

Pop held up a hand. "That was different."

"How so?"

Hues of red and orange from the bonfire flickered over Pop's face. He kneaded the back of his neck as his eyes roved over the acres stretching out around them.

"Gloria never wanted to come here. Raintree was always my dream, not hers. She tolerated it because she loved me but she wanted something different." His mouth twisted. "And she found someone else that would give it to her."

Logan sighed. "We were better off without her, any-way."

"You think so?" Pop glanced at him. "I wanted your mother from the first moment I saw her, but we both knew we weren't a good match. She was happy in the city and I was a rancher just passing through." A short bark of laughter escaped him. "That short skirt and high heels of hers did me in, though. I fought it but it didn't take long for the rest of her to win me over, too. We knew the odds were stacked against us but we loved each other enough to give it a shot." His smile dissolved. "She ended up being miserable here and wanted to go back to her old life. I tried my best to talk her into stay-ing. It didn't work out because neither of us was willing to give up one path for the other."

Logan scoffed. "Except her path had another man on it."

"Not at first. But she did meet him and she ended up choosing a life with him instead of here with us. Wasn't much I could do about it and still keep my dig-nity. There are things in life you can't control, Logan. At least, your mother was honest. Told me how she felt before she acted on it."

"And that excuses it?"

"No." Pop's tone turned sharp. "It was one thing to walk out on me. But my boys—" He swallowed hard and looked away. "I wasn't proud of myself back then. No matter how much I hated your mother for leaving y'all, I still loved that woman in equal measure. Prob-ably always will. And that's how it is. You don't get to pick who you fall in love with. It just happens. If it works out, you end up living with 'em. If it doesn't," he said, and shrugged slowly, "you find a way to live without 'em. It took me a long time to learn that."

Logan dropped his head, focusing on the shadows cast by the bonfire.

"Guess that's why I've never blamed Amy for going after you like she did," Pop said. "I knew what it felt like to want someone that much. That girl's always had a strong spirit and loved you the second she laid eyes on you. As hard as it may be to understand, she was just fighting to keep you."

Pop's hand curled around his forearm. Logan tensed, lifting his eyes to face him.

"I wish you'd open up for once. Tell me what you're thinking. Feeling. You're closed so tight—" He kicked the ground with a boot. "But that's my fault. I put too much on you when your mama took off. Left you to tend to your brother. I had so much trouble holding myself together I didn't realize how much you boys needed me."

"We turned out fine, Pop."

"Fine's not good enough. Not for me or my boys. You've always been careful and independent. Even as a kid. But sometimes living safe keeps you from the best things in life." Pop watched Amy disappear into the darkness, then peered back at him. "Amy used to enjoy life. Showed you how to at one time. She could be the best thing that ever happened to you." His grip tightened on Logan's arm. "But if you want a real shot at saving your marriage, you've got to open up."

"I'm trying."

"No, you're not." He shook his head. "You're pushing Amy away like you do the rest of us because you're afraid of things going bad." He hesitated. "You've gotten worse since y'all lost the baby."

The baby. Logan's muscles tensed. *A mistake.* "Her name was Sara."

"I'm sorry," Pop murmured, touching his arm. "You haven't been the same since you lost Sara. And it's time for you to…"

"What?"

Pop sighed. "Move on. You've spent so much time worrying about Amy, it's time you worked on yourself. Time for you to let go of what happened. Time to forget—"

"Forget Sara?" Logan's throat closed, tightening to the point of pain.

Pop winced. "No. I didn't mean that."

"That's exactly what you meant." Logan's gut roiled. "And that should be easy, right? Because I'm a man? Because I didn't know her? That's the same thing everyone else said after we lost her."

"Logan—"

"I knew my daughter." His voice turned hoarse, tearing from his throat in rough rasps. "Sara knew me, too. I put my hand on Amy's belly every day and Sara kicked every time I spoke to her." His breath shuddered from him. "That's how I knew something wasn't right. I put my hand over her that morning and talked to her and she didn't move." He shook his head. "Amy didn't think anything was wrong. Not until later. But I knew that morning."

Logan stared ahead, the flames of the bonfire licking higher and the smoke growing thicker.

"We'd lost her that night while we were sleeping." His lungs seized, choking him. "Sara died right there in that bed beside me and I couldn't do a damned thing about it."

"No one expected you to, son. Nature has a way—"

"Of taking care of things. I know." Logan grimaced, eyes blurring. "That's why I can't understand it. When we saw her, she was beautiful. So perfect. She just didn't cry." He shoved his trembling hands in his pockets. "I kept holding her, thinking they'd got it wrong. That she'd wake up. She would've been due in two more weeks. I can't understand how she could be that perfect and not cry. How she could *almost* make it…"

Pop kneaded the back of Logan's neck, his words low against his ear. "It's okay to mourn for Sara. To miss her. But it wasn't your fault or Amy's. You have to accept this was something you couldn't control and choose to move on. For your sake and hers."

"Every choice I've ever made has been for Amy's sake." Logan pulled away. "It's called loyalty. Something a lot stronger than this illusion of love everyone keeps holding on to. It's something Mom knew nothing about. Even Amy didn't have a clue what it was, lying to me the way she did. And I have no intention of trading it off for this reckless fantasy all of you keep trying to sell. The only thing that's ever been certain in my life has been my word. Everything else—*everyone* else— has been a damned disappointment." He motioned to the hands across the field and called out, "Let's get this fire out. It's time to call it a night."

They nodded, tossing their beers in the trash and rounding up buckets of water.

"Logan, you can't build a future when your hands are holding on to the past."

"The only thing I'm holding on to is my wife. I made a vow and I'm standing by it because it's the right thing to do." His lip curled. "The only *dignified* thing to do.

Surely you can understand that." He shook his head. "Amy and I may have been dumb kids back then but we're not now. I'm not going into this blind, and Amy knows exactly where I stand." His mouth ran dry and he forced his words past the lump in his throat. "I knew my daughter. Sara was not *a mistake*. And neither was my marriage."

Logan spun on his heel and joined the hands, grabbing a bucket of water and heaving it over the pit. The hiss and sizzle of dying fire sounded and smoke billowed out with fury. He grabbed another and repeated the motion, muscles screaming with every throw.

Things would be different this time. He wouldn't fail Amy. And thank God they'd never have the chance to fail a child again.

"Mmmm." Amy closed her eyes in bliss and wrapped her hands tighter around the warm mug. "Mama, you make the best hot chocolate in existence."

Betty smiled. "It's all about balance, baby girl. You have to make sure the bitter matches the sweet. Besides, you can't break in Christmas properly without a decent hot cocoa."

Amy took another sip and rolled it over her tongue, savoring the peaceful stillness of the empty kitchen. She and Traci had helped Cissy get the boys bathed and tucked in bed. Traci and Cissy had called it a night but Amy had lingered, reading three bedtime stories before the boys' eyelids finally fluttered shut.

Amy smiled. She could've stayed in the boys' room for hours, reading in gentle tones and listening to their soft breaths. It hadn't taken long for their rambunctious sweetness to slip into her heart. She'd grown so close to them it'd be painful to leave.

Betty set her cup down and reached across the table to squeeze Amy's forearm. "It's good to see you smile again."

Amy drummed her fingers against her cup. "I smile enough. Matter of fact, we have plenty of laughs when you and Traci visit me in Augusta."

Betty shook her head. "They're not like the ones you had out by the bonfire tonight. You looked like your old self again wearing Logan's hat and grinning. I don't know what he did to coax it out of you but he did it right."

Amy's face flamed. She sat back, dodging Betty's narrowed gaze. "We went for a ride, is all. I just haven't ridden in so long it was nice to race again. I forgot how much I enjoyed it."

Betty released her arm and retrieved her cup. Amy dug into the plastic bag of marshmallows on the table, plucked one out and plopped it into her cocoa. It bobbed around in the dark liquid, melting in white streaks around the edges.

She pressed the cup to her lips and the sickly-sweet foam of the melted marshmallow clung to her gums, rolling her stomach. She dropped the mug to the table with a clang and pressed the back of her hand to her mouth.

"Are you okay?" Betty leaned forward, brow creasing.

Amy nodded and swallowed. "Yeah. I haven't been feeling well, lately."

Her hand shook. Betty's gaze clung to it. Amy shoved it between her knees below the table.

"Baby, you know you can come to me for anything, right? No matter how old you are?"

"I know."

"Well, I'm here if you ever want to talk." Betty shifted forward, mouth opening and closing a time or two. "About your new job or the move." She shrugged, fiddling with the handle on her cup. "Or Logan."

Amy's lips twitched. "Smooth delivery, Mama. Real smooth."

Betty flushed and waved a hand in front of her face. "I forget you have so much of your father in you." She smiled. "He never had much use for tact, either."

Amy laughed, the churning in her gut easing. Betty was right. Her dad had always been blunt. They reminisced about his many missteps and before long, Betty joined her, doubling over and holding her belly as she chuckled. At the same time, Betty's eyes darkened with sadness over the loss of her husband.

The nausea returned and Amy's laughter broke away, fading with each jerk of her shoulders. Amy fought for air, her lungs burning. She pressed a weak fist to her chest, fighting to regain composure at Betty's shocked expression.

"I'm scared, Mama."

Betty moved quickly to the seat beside Amy and hugged her close. "Of what?"

Possibly being pregnant. Losing another child. Losing Logan. Her throat closed and violent chills racked her body.

"Try to relax, Amy."

Betty's voice trembled. Her hand moved in warm circles over Amy's back, slowing as the spasms subsided and resting between her shoulder blades.

"Now, what is it you're afraid of?"

"Everything," Amy whispered. "Leaving. Staying." She clamped her trembling lips together. "*Myself.* I don't know who I am anymore."

Betty smoothed her fingers through Amy's hair, tucking a long wave behind her shoulder. Amy leaned into her, craving the soothing touch as much as she had when she was a child.

"Maybe that's because you're trying to be someone you're not," Betty murmured, gesturing toward Amy's necklace. "When did you take that ring off your finger and string it around your neck?"

Amy bit her lip. "What does that have to do with anything?"

"Everything." Betty squeezed her hand. "I know losing Sara was difficult. I knew you needed to heal and I thought leaving here for a change of pace was the best thing for you at the time." She shook her head. "But you carried it with you."

Amy licked her lips, the taste of salt lingering on her tongue.

Betty grabbed a cloth napkin from the table and dabbed at Amy's cheeks. "I think you've been so determined to get some distance from the bad that you forgot about the good."

"What good?" A scornful laugh burst past Amy's lips. "Not one single thing I did was good. I lied. I hurt Logan. Not to mention Sara—" Her voice broke. She stilled Betty's hand, taking the napkin and wiping her eyes. "But I've been trying to be someone good. Someone better. What's wrong with that?"

"Nothing," Betty whispered. "So long as you remember that no one can be perfect no matter how hard they try. We're, none of us, saints or angels. We all make mistakes." She tugged Amy's hands to her lap and eyed her. "If you don't mind my asking, who is it you're really doing all this changing for?"

Amy ducked her head and picked at the hem of her shirt. "Logan, I suppose."

Betty sighed. "I know I should be objective right now. Tell you how proud I am of you for being so repentant and selfless." She slid closer, smile tight. "But I won't. You're my girl, Amy, and I'm proud of you. Always have been. I'd hate to see you change the things I love most about you to impress a man. Even if he is a good one."

"There's more to it than that."

"Is there?" Betty asked. "You used to like who you were and were proud of it. You were so brave and headstrong." She smiled. "I remember watching you fall off a horse more times than I could count. Was scared to death you'd hurt yourself. But you'd get right back up, brush yourself off and try again. Every time. And you kept on trying until you got it right."

"Or got it wrong," Amy choked out. "I kept right after Logan, too, and look how that ended up."

Betty took Amy's hands in hers and squeezed. "You've always lived hard and you love just as hard. Your heart was in the right place no matter how wrong you went about it. Your daddy was the same way and you remind me so much of him. That's why it's so hard for me to let you go." Her eyes watered. "I'm not going to lie to you. I don't want you to move so far away. But I do want you to be happy. If that means moving to Michigan then I'll support you. Traci and I will visit you just as we've been doing." Her features firmed.

"But no matter what you decide, I won't help you hide yourself away. I love you too much to support you in that." She tapped a finger against the ring at Amy's neck. "That one mistake has been weighing you down long enough. It's past time to set it down, forgive yourself and live again."

The tension in Amy's muscles eased, the tightness seeping away and leaving a soothing stillness in its place. She hugged Betty, absorbing her strength.

"Now." Betty squeezed Amy close. "How 'bout I sneak us a few sugar cookies and we pile on the couch and watch a late movie together like we used to?"

Amy sniffed and smiled. "I'd like that."

They stayed up and watched the last hour of one of their favorite holiday comedies, nibbling on cookies and sharing laughs. Betty's eyes grew heavy and Amy kissed her cheek, suggesting it was time to turn in.

Betty paused at the door and smiled. "You're loved, Amy. No matter where you are or what you do. I wasn't the only one that loved the girl you used to be. Logan did, too. And would again if you'd give him half a chance."

Standing motionless in the living room, Amy watched her mother leave. The house was quiet. All the guests had turned in for the night and Logan would be coming in soon. A steady ticking from the clock on the wall marked the time, bringing the future closer in small moments that weighed on her shoulders.

Amy glanced down at her boots. They were as banged up and muddied as they'd been when she'd run reckless as a teen. They felt as comforting now as they did back then. As if she could bound effortlessly across the ground with every step.

She wondered if the girl she'd been then was still inside her, the good and the bad in equal measure. She continued to ponder this long after she'd crawled into bed.

Logan joined her soon after, wrapping his arms around her and falling asleep. The gentle rhythm of his breathing offered comfort but sleep escaped her. She eventually gave up and slipped out of his arms, dressing and leaving the room quietly.

It was dark save for the light of the stars as she made her way to the stables. The path seemed to stretch farther than ever in the chill of the night air. She stopped more than once, almost turning back, but continued to put one boot in front of the other until she reached Thunder's stall and placed her palm to the bars.

"Hey," she whispered.

Thunder's dark bulk shifted. He stomped a time or two and tossed his head.

"Not getting any sleep, either, huh?" Amy smiled. "Want to come with me? Take a night stroll like we used to and stretch your legs?"

He kicked, hooves striking the stall door. The sharp crack of wood split her ears. Amy held her ground, keeping her hand flat against the bars.

Thunder kicked again then paced, growing calmer and slowly approaching her hand. His nose drew closer, nostrils moving rapidly with strong pulls of air.

"Remember me?" Her throat closed and her vision blurred. "Because I think I need you to."

He nudged closer, his wet nose and swift breaths tickling her skin. She reached with slow movements for the lead rope hanging on the wall.

"We'll take it one step at a time," she whispered. "Until we trust each other again. That okay with you?"

Thunder tossed his head and pawed the ground but she managed to get the lead on him and move him to the round pen. She slipped the rope off him once they made it inside the enclosure. He took off, bucking and kicking at the fence.

Her heart pounded against her ribs but she pushed on and walked him back several times, moving through the familiar routine and feeling the strength return to her trembling legs.

"Easy," she murmured, lifting her arms.

The glow from the starlit sky pooled over him. His dark mane ruffled with each push of the wind. He tossed his head up, crying and stomping the ground, eyes flaring with fear.

Amy's arms grew heavy but she kept them up, palms out. "I'm here," she whispered. "Right here. Whenever you're ready."

Thunder pinned his ears and ducked his head.

"I'm right here," she repeated.

Her body quaked. She closed her eyes, the lump in her throat tightening. Thunder's hoof hit the ground, the solid thud disturbing the stillness of the night, and his heavy pulls of air rasped across the distance between them.

It was silent for a moment. Then the familiar pounding of hooves sounded.

Amy tensed as the rapid slams increased in speed, growing closer. She opened her eyes, pushed her arms higher and advanced, pushing him back.

Thunder cut right, sweeping back with heavy stomps. His cry slashed through the air, piercing her ears. He tossed his head then nestled against the fence and stilled.

Amy waited for several minutes then advanced slowly toward his hip. Thunder jerked as she touched his back but stilled when she moved her palm over him with soothing whispers. His breathing slowed and Amy's followed the same, calm rhythm, her breath passing past her lips in white puffs on the frigid air.

"I'm sorry," she rasped.

Her throat tightened, cutting off the sound, and tears scalded her cheeks. The cry echoed inside her. It burned her chest, leaving her gasping and mouthing the soundless words.

I'm sorry.

And God help her, she was. Sorry for Thunder's pain. For betraying Logan. For every day that passed without her beautiful daughter in it.

Her arms dropped, her hands clutching her middle, and she cried. For Sara. For Logan. For the girl she used to be. And what could have been.

She didn't notice how much time passed. Didn't realize when the tears finally stopped. But the knot in her chest untied and her shoulders sagged with sweet release. The kind she hadn't known in years. A sense of peace. A welling of hope and forgiveness. Silent comforts that had escaped her for so long.

Thunder remained still, head lowered and body relaxed.

"I'm right here," Amy whispered. "Whenever you're ready."

She began walking, moving slowly along the curve of the fence and rounding the pen. The wind slowed to a gentle breeze and she inhaled, the clean air filling her lungs and refreshing her spirit.

It was on the ninth pass that Thunder followed. He took hesitant steps at her back but kept time with her, matching her step for step.

They completed one lap. Then another and another until Amy lost count. The only reminder of their efforts was the sheen of sweat collecting beneath her shirt and coating Thunder's hide.

The air warmed and a hint of red peeked above the horizon. Dawn approached and the tendrils of sunlight had never looked so bright or felt so warm. Amy stopped, soaking in the glow of the sun.

Something warm and wet nuzzled her palm. Thunder's broad head nudged her arm up. Smiling, she turned and looped her arms around his neck, pressing her forehead to his warm neck and praising him.

Thunder's heat spread to her belly. A gentle throb pulsed in her veins, flowing through her blood and pooling in her middle. She knew the feeling. Recognized it immediately, even though she hadn't experienced it in years.

It lit her up on the inside, fighting off the frigid air and blazing bright in her chest. She was hopeful. And that feeling was strong. More all-consuming than ever.

Amy smiled, wrapping her arms tighter around Thunder's neck, holding on to it all and savoring every delicious thrill. The hope of a miracle. Another chance at being a mother.

The sweet promise of the future had never felt this good before. And she knew the only reason it did now was because she'd felt the bad.

"Are you tired, boy?"

Thunder snorted, nudging her with his nose.

She laughed. "Neither am I. Wanna run? Like we used to?"

She left the rope behind, exited the pen and left the gate open for Thunder to join her. Amy gripped his withers and made to jump but a strong pair of hands wrapped around her waist.

"That's my girl." Logan's deep tenor rumbled at her back as he lifted her.

Amy settled astride Thunder and glanced down. "How long have you been out here?"

"Long enough." He looked up at her, his dark eyes warm and tender.

"Well, I'll be damned."

Dominic stood several feet behind Logan. The boys stood on either side of him, bulky coats zipped up and wide smiles across their faces.

"Yeah," Kayden drawled, crossing his arms like Dominic, "I'll be damned."

Dominic cringed and clamped a hand over Kayden's mouth, sneaking a peek over his shoulder. "All right, now. Don't say that around your aunt Cissy."

Amy laughed, the sound bursting from her chest and mingling with Logan's. Jayden ran over to beam up at Thunder.

"Is he happy now, Aunt Amy?"

She nodded. "He will be."

Logan lifted Jayden. "Give him a good pet. Your aunt Amy's gonna take him out for a while."

Jayden patted Thunder's neck, smiled and whispered, "Thanks for making him happy, Aunt Amy."

She returned Jayden's smile with her own. In that

moment, the bitter in her life was balanced with the perfect amount of sweet. The kind of sweet promise she deserved to hold on to. Even if it meant letting Logan go.

Chapter Nine

"Blue wrapping paper, silver ribbons, name tags, cowboy hats and—"

"A partridge in a pear tree?" Amy winked as Traci dumped a pile of shopping bags on the wide leather couch in the family room.

"No, but if the store sold 'em, I'm sure Dominic would've bought those, too." Traci puffed a strand of dark hair out of her eyes. "He settled for a trampoline instead."

"A trampoline?" Cissy's blond head shot up. Her hands froze over the present she wrapped, a bit of tape clinging to her fingertips.

Amy grinned. The past few days had flown by in a flurry of shopping, wrapping and hiding. She'd helped Cissy hide more Santa presents for the boys in two days than she could remember receiving over all her childhood years put together. Since it was Christmas Eve and stores closed early, Cissy had felt it safe enough to send Dominic out for more wrapping supplies without him returning with another armful of toys.

"Now, don't get upset, baby." Dominic edged sideways through the living room door, his dimpled smile as wide as the load of firewood weighing down his arms.

Cissy frowned. "I asked you to get more wrapping paper, not more gifts. At this rate, there won't be enough gift wrap in the world to cover the boys' presents."

Undeterred, Dominic dumped the wood in a basket by the blazing fireplace and crossed the room to kiss Cissy's forehead.

"It's Christmas," he murmured, smoothing a hand through her hair. "Only comes once a year."

"But you're spoiling them, Dominic." Cissy flushed, eyes fluttering shut as he feathered more kisses to her cheeks and the tip of her nose.

"Mmm-hmm. Gonna spoil my girls, too." He placed a gentle hand over her belly. "Anyway, I didn't buy the hats. That was all Logan's doing."

Logan walked in, holding a couple of thick oak logs. "I didn't see anything wrong with buying my nephews one more present. The boys have been good this year." His brow furrowed and a crooked grin broke out across his face. "For most of it, anyway."

Cissy sighed, blue eyes dancing. "You'd think two big, muscle-bound men could stand up to a couple of little boys. Turns out, you and Dom are the biggest push-overs in existence."

Amy laughed. Logan's dark eyes locked with hers.

"That," Logan murmured, "we might be."

Amy looked away and shifted closer to the lamp-light at her side. She concentrated on slipping flannel shirts into boxes for the boys and savored the gentle flutters in her belly.

Since her breakthrough with Thunder, she and Logan had taken the stallion out for a ride every day over the past week. During which, Logan had sweet-talked her into several more races and a dozen years' worth of kisses.

She glanced up as Logan crossed to the fireplace and stowed the logs in the basket. A few strategic turns of wood with the poker and he had the fire flaming high again. The red flames and glow of yellow light accentuated his muscular profile.

Amy pulled the gift boxes closer to her belly and tried to calm the tremors running over her skin. *Four weeks.* It'd been four weeks now since they'd made love and her hopes of a possible pregnancy had grown stronger than ever.

Despite her excitement, she hadn't been able to follow through with confirming it. The past week with Logan had been especially sweet and she wanted to hold on to it. They smiled and laughed together often. They'd become more than best friends again. Only, she wasn't quite sure what they'd become.

She knew Logan was aware she loved him. But she'd never heard it from him and it was time to face the possibility that she never would. Friendship was the strongest bond he offered.

Logan turned, his expression cast in darkness by the flames at his back, his face as difficult to read as his carefully controlled emotions.

How would he handle the news of another pregnancy? He'd made it clear that he didn't believe it was possible for them to have another child. And four years ago, he'd reminded her of how dangerous a pregnancy would be every time he'd given in to her persuasions.

Amy curled her fingers around the corners of the gift boxes in her lap. Back then, things had played out exactly as Logan had predicted. They'd had no luck conceiving. But now...

Now, there was a real chance. She stilled her bouncing knee. As excited as she was, she was equally dismayed. She wanted Logan, but having him out of obligation was no longer something she could accept. She needed more than loyalty and so would their child.

"Sustenance for Santa's elves," Betty chimed.

Betty and Pop entered with trays of hot chocolate and set two red mugs in front of Amy and Cissy.

"Bless you," Cissy murmured, picking up her cup and sipping.

Traci and Dominic each grabbed a mug and plopped down on the floor in front of the fireplace. It was quiet for a few minutes, save for the snap and crackle of the wood burning. They sipped their sweet beverages and watched the flames burn brighter.

An additional crackle sounded at Amy's back. She frowned, glancing over her shoulder to find four small hands reaching over the arm of the couch and digging around in the shopping bags.

"Boys," Amy whispered, "there's no peeking at Christmas."

Their blond heads popped over the arm of the couch and two pairs of wide blue eyes blinked at her.

"Oh, for goodness' sakes," Cissy grumbled. "Haven't I told you two to stay out of this room until tomorrow morning? Santa's going to fly right over the ranch if he finds out you've been sneaking into presents early."

Both boys jumped out from behind the couch and held up their hands.

"We ain't took nothing, Aunt Cissy," Kayden said. "Promise."

Cissy sighed. "You mean you *haven't taken any-thing*."

"That's right." Kayden nodded, his face scrunching up with confusion. "I ain't took nothing." He turned to his brother. "Did you?"

"Uh-uh," Jayden protested, waving around his empty hands. "We ain't took nothing, Aunt Cissy."

Cissy smiled and shook her head. "I give up."

They all laughed. Logan walked to the couch and rummaged around in the bags, a slow smile lifting his cheeks.

"Well, you're in luck, boys," he said, pulling out two small cowboy hats. "These, you can have now."

The boys whooped and jumped around, barely holding still long enough for Logan to settle a tan hat on each of their heads.

"What do you say?" Cissy asked.

"Thank you, Uncle Logan," they both chimed, hugging his legs.

Kayden strutted away to stand beside Dominic, poked his chest out and propped his hands on his hips. "We're bone-a-fine cowboys now, Uncle Dominic. Like you, Uncle Logan and Mr. Jed."

Traci snorted. "Like I keep telling you squirts, it's *bona fide*."

"That's what I said," Kayden argued.

The bag rattled again. Jayden burrowed around in it. "There's another one, Uncle Logan. Who gets it?"

Logan reached over Jayden and tugged out a black straw hat. A row of silver-toned rhinestones circled the band, giving it a classic, stylish look.

"This one's for your aunt Amy," Logan said, placing it on her head. His broad hands moved over the brim, bending and shaping the edges. His narrowed eyes roved over her face as he adjusted the hat then stilled with satisfaction. "Beautiful."

"Thank you," she whispered.

Logan nudged the brim up and kissed her. "You're welcome. Thought it was time you had one of your own."

"You're a real cowgirl now, Aunt Amy." Jayden beamed with pride. "You got a hat and everything."

Amy smiled. "I suppose so."

"It's stunning," Cissy said. "Don't you think so, Betty?"

Betty beamed. "It's gorgeous." She blinked rapidly, gathering up the dirty mugs and pausing on her way out. "You boys better get ready for bed if you want Santa to drop by."

The twins darted to the window, shoved aside the curtains and peered out.

"Is he on the way now?" Jayden asked.

"Will be soon," Cissy said.

"What'd you ask Santa for, Aunt Cissy?" Kayden scampered over, placing his hands on Cissy's knees and leaning in.

Cissy winked and rubbed her belly. "Your baby cousins, Grace and Gwen."

Kayden scowled. "Is that all?"

Dominic laughed. "You'll think differently once they get here. You'll be like their big brother." He nodded at Logan. "Someone they can look up to."

Amy's chest swelled as the Slade men shared a smile. It was wonderful seeing them so close again. It seemed Dominic's return to Raintree had worked all sorts of magic on the family. A magic she was beginning to feel herself.

Jayden looked thoughtful then whispered something in Kayden's ear. He seemed to agree and the two took off, clutching their new hats to their heads.

"Best get them to bed, pronto." Dominic moved toward the door. "Looks like they're up to something."

"I'll give you a hand." Pop laughed, following him out of the room.

"All right," Cissy said, "I think we deserve a break. Thanks for the help with the shopping, Logan. We never would've gotten it done without your help."

"No problem." Logan grinned. "Why don't you get a bite to eat? I'll get the other presents out of the truck. The wrapping can wait. I have a feeling it'll be a while before Dom gets the boys settled."

Right on cue, the twins barreled back into the room, shoving past Amy and Traci toward the fireplace. They carried a large bucket between them and sloshed water onto the hardwood floor with every step.

"What in the world?" Cissy murmured.

"Hold up there, boys," Dominic shouted, rushing in behind them.

It was too late. Kayden and Jayden dumped the entire contents of the bucket onto the fire, killing it with a sizzle and sending billows of black smoke into the room.

Amy shut her eyes and waved a hand in front of her face, the mass of smoke choking the air from the room. Violent bouts of coughing sounded as she grappled her way over to the window. She struggled to unlatch the lock, the dark clouds of smoke making it difficult to see.

Logan's big hand covered hers, unlocking the window and heaving it open with a shove. Amy took off her hat and waved it wildly, ushering the smoke outside and blinking as it cleared.

Dominic stood by the fireplace. Each of his hands clutched a twin by the waistband, holding them in the air.

"Why did you do that?" Dominic sputtered as he shook them gently. "I know I won't understand but go ahead and tell me. Why?"

Jayden scrunched his nose and twisted his head up to answer, "So Grace and Gwen won't get hurt."

Dominic blinked. "What?"

"That's what Aunt Cissy asked Santa for." Kayden squirmed against Dominic's hold. "The fire's hot and the babies will get hurt when he comes down the chimney with 'em. So, we had to put it out."

Dominic's face went slack and he burst into laughter. Amy joined him, dropping her hat to the window-sill and glancing over at a chuckling Logan.

Cissy shook her head. "We talked about this, boys. The babies won't come for a few more weeks. I thought you understood the babies were in here," she said, patting her belly.

Amy's heart tripped as she studied Logan's profile. A muscle in his jaw ticked and his posture grew rigid.

The boys cocked their heads and studied Cissy's belly with a frown.

"So you asked Santa for 'em, he made 'em and then put 'em in there?" Jayden asked.

"No," Kayden declared, smacking a hand on his brother's arm. "Santa don't do all that. That's what the elves are for." He glanced up at Dominic. "Ain't that how babies are made?"

Dominic cleared his throat "Not exactly."

"Then how?" Kayden asked. "How are babies made?"

"Go ahead, Dominic," Cissy said, laughing. "Explain it to us."

Amy slipped her hand in Logan's. He glanced at her, smile tight and eyes bitter.

Her chest ached. There was no way Logan would react well to the news of a possible pregnancy. The pain of losing Sara was plain in his expression.

"Amy?" Logan squeezed her hand, his deep voice low against her ear. He studied her, his face creased with concern. "You okay? You went pale there for a second."

She leaned her head out of the window and sucked in a lungful of icy air. "I'm fine. Just took in a little too much smoke, I guess."

"See there, boys," Dominic boomed, "you owe Aunt Amy an apology."

"Are you avoiding the question, Dominic?" Cissy asked.

Dominic chuckled. "No. I'll be more than happy to explain it to you tonight, baby. In the meantime, you boys go apologize to your aunt Amy, then help me clean up this mess."

The boys ran across the room and tugged at Amy's jeans.

"Sorry, Aunt Amy," Kayden said.

"Me, too," Jayden added.

Grateful for the distraction, Amy knelt and drew the boys close. They wrapped their arms around her and pecked a kiss to her cheeks.

"Y'all better be on your best behavior for the rest of the night," Logan said. "So Santa doesn't hold it against you."

"We will," the boys chimed, nuzzling their warm faces into Amy's neck.

Logan scooped up Amy's hat from the window-sill and placed it back on her head. His warm palm smoothed through her hair and curled around her shoulder, causing her heart to beat faster.

"Santa won't be mad with us," Jayden whispered against her ear. "It's all right 'cuz everything turned out okay. Right, Aunt Amy?"

Amy hugged the boys close against her middle, spirits lifting at the thought of comforting her own child in her arms. A possibility that became more real with each passing day.

"Yeah," she whispered. "Everything's okay."

It would be. Either way. Life was moving on and there was a chance things might change. That she might become a mother, after all.

She hugged the boys tighter, straightened her hat with her other hand and smiled. It was the time of year for gifts. And the smallest ones, it seemed, held the biggest promise of all.

"HE CAME!"

Logan jumped, eyes flying open and arms clutching Amy tighter to his chest. The mattress beneath him dipped to one side then bounced. The springs squeaked and the bed frame rattled.

"Santa came!" Kayden jumped up and down at the end of the bed. "He ate all the cookies we left and he drank all the milk and—"

"He left presents," Jayden shouted, scrambling onto the bed and bouncing with his brother. "Lots and lots of presents! They're under the tree and in the hallway and in our room—"

"And he left a trampoline outside," Kayden gasped. He stopped jumping and dropped to Logan's chest, his small knees jabbing into Logan's ribs. "A trampoline, Uncle Logan!" His face contorted. He raised his fists and shook them on a primal yell. "A *tram-po-line*!"

Logan winced, his voice leaving him on a painful groan. "Then why aren't you using it instead of me?"

Gentle breaths of laughter brushed his ear, causing the skin on his neck to tighten. He rolled his head to the side. Amy smiled up at him, green eyes warm and excited. Her cheeks flushed a sweet shade of pink and her raven hair clung to her face in mussed waves.

Logan's chest warmed. Christmas morning was definitely much more beautiful with Amy at his side. Friends, like they used to be. The relationship familiar, safe and inviting.

He cleared his throat, leaning in and whispering, "Merry Chr—"

"Come on, Uncle Logan," Kayden said, smooshing his hands against Logan's cheeks. He leaned in, the tip of his nose brushing Logan's. "Get up. Aunt Cissy said we can't open presents until everyone's up."

"Yeah, get up, Aunt Amy," Jayden hollered, tugging at Amy's nightshirt.

"Boys, I told you to keep your tails out of here." Dom stuck his head inside the room, his hand covering his eyes. "You two decent, I hope?"

Amy laughed and Logan joined her.

"Yep," he said.

Dominic dropped his hand and smiled, dimples

flashing. "Then get your butts out here and let's get this party started."

Five minutes later, Logan and Amy were dressed and in the family room. The boys pounced on the presents while the adults sipped warm drinks and watched with smiles. The next several hours passed in a blur of squeals, torn wrapping paper and excited hugs.

It didn't take long for Logan to get swept up in the twin tornado. He, Pop and Dominic assembled new gadgets for the boys and helped them test out their new toys. It had taken the boys over an hour to tear into them all. Then, they spent hour upon hour afterward testing out each one. At one point, the boys couldn't decide whether to eat or play. They ended up grabbing a handful of sugar cookies, eating them with one hand and shooting their toy guns with the other.

Eventually, Logan crashed into a heap on the floor. His eyes grew heavy as they lingered on Amy but even her delighted smile couldn't keep the exhaustion at bay.

"Logan."

A hushed whisper swept by his ear, the sweetest voice he'd ever heard calling his name.

"Logan."

The familiar scent of strawberries lingered on the air. A long sweep of hair poured over his shoulder and gentle lips touched his cheek. Logan opened his eyes to find Amy leaning over him. Those emerald eyes of hers more gorgeous than ever under the wide brim of her black hat. They trailed over his face, heating his skin and causing his heart to trip in his chest.

"I hate to wake you," she whispered with a smile. "But it's getting late."

Logan blinked, focusing on her expression. The same

sweet one she'd first given him so long ago. Full of hope and admiration.

He shifted, lifting his arms to pull her close and claim her mouth but his elbows were glued to the floor.

Amy laughed and glanced at either side of him. "They're knocked out, too. You've all had a long day."

Logan turned his head to find Kayden draped face-down over his left arm and Jayden sprawled on his back over his right one. They clutched half-eaten peppermint sticks in their hands, each rhythmic snore puffing between their sticky red lips and brushing over his chest.

Logan smiled. He'd fallen asleep and, apparently, the boys had joined him. Amy was right. It had been a long Christmas day. Full of fun, food and family. And, of course, gifts. He lifted his head off the floor and scanned the mountains of torn wrapping paper, piles of toys and scattered ribbons littering the family room.

Presents. Logan chuckled. There'd been acres of them.

"Where is everyone?" he asked, clearing his throat to erase the husky note from his voice.

"Cissy was worn out so Dom and I sent her to bed. Dom and Pop are checking the stables, Mama and Traci are watching a Christmas movie marathon in the living room." Amy winked. "And the partridge is still in the pear tree."

Logan's smile stretched his cheeks. Lord, she was beautiful. He wanted to tell her. Wanted to tug her close. Hold on to her and the moment.

"Come on," she whispered, sliding her hands under Jayden's arms, "it's time to put our nephews to bed."

Our. Dear God, he wanted…

He caught her elbow as she lifted Jayden off his arm. "Hey."

She paused and glanced at him, expression expectant. He swallowed hard.

"Merry Christmas," he whispered.

She grinned, the pink flush of her cheeks causing his body to tighten. "Merry Christmas."

Jayden grumbled as she lifted him upright and held his hat to his head. Logan rolled to a seated position, then tugged Kayden to his chest and stood. He made swift work of settling a twin on each hip and they made their way quietly down the hall and into the boys' bedroom.

Amy took the boys' hats off and hung them on the bedposts, then motioned Logan into the bathroom. She wet a washcloth with warm water and he held the boys while she gently wiped away the sticky peppermint and scrubbed a toothbrush over their teeth to the tune of their sleepy grumbles.

Soon, they'd put each of them into their beds and tucked the covers snug around them. Logan bent and placed a kiss on Jayden's forehead. Amy did the same for Kayden.

"Aunt Amy?"

Logan stopped, watching as Amy tiptoed back to Kayden's bed.

"What is it, baby?" she asked, smoothing a hand over his blond curls.

"Can I sleep with my hat on?"

"Of course, you can." She plucked it off the bedpost and placed it gently on his head. "There. You're a bone-a-fine cowboy even when you sleep."

"And you're a real cowgirl," Jayden murmured sleepily, pointing to her hat.

"Dang sure am," she said.

The boys giggled.

Kayden curled his arms around Amy's neck, tugging her close. "I love you, Aunt Amy."

"Me, too," Jayden murmured.

Logan's chest clenched, a warm ache spreading over him and making him catch his breath. She hugged Kayden, a gentle smile appearing.

"I love both of you, too," she whispered, kissing Kayden's nose then Jayden's. "Very much."

The boys hunkered down under the covers, eyed each other, then sang out with sleepy smiles, "Merry Christmas."

Amy laughed. "Merry Christmas. Now you two go to sleep."

"Yes, ma'am," they whispered, snuggling into their pillows.

She tucked the blankets a little tighter around them and left the room. Logan followed her into the hallway, pulling the door closed behind him. Her long legs carried her farther away, that beautiful raven hair of hers swinging across her back.

Logan fisted his hands at his sides, his body shaking. "Amy?"

She stopped walking and turned, the wide brim of her hat skimming the curves of her dark eyebrows and casting a shadow over her mouth.

"I want..." His throat closed.

He wanted her. Wanted her so much it scared the hell out of him. Made him lose his logic and good sense.

"I want to..."

Hold her every night. See her first thing every morning. Have her in his life every day.

"To wish me Merry Christmas again?" she teased, crossing her arms under her full breasts. "I seem to be getting a lot of those lately."

Logan shook his head. He took long strides across the floor, wrapped his hands around her hips and nudged her against the wall.

Those gorgeous green eyes of hers softened. "What is it you want, Logan?"

He swallowed hard, shoved down the lump in his throat and pressed close. "I want you to stay," he whispered. "For good."

His heart raced and his hands trembled. The ache in his chest grew, becoming intense and all-consuming. He steadied his hands around her hips and slipped his leg between hers, striving for control. Hating this weakness. This dependency on her.

Her brows lifted and moisture sheened her eyes. She asked hesitantly, "You do?"

Logan nodded, touching a kiss to her mouth.

"Why?" she whispered.

He ducked his head, pressing his hot cheek to her cool one, then trailed his mouth down her neck, nipping and kissing. She softened beneath him, her arms sliding over his back and sweet moans escaping her.

"Logan." She tugged his head up and drifted a fingertip over the seam of his mouth. "Tell me. Why do you want me to stay?"

He firmed his jaw. "Because you're my wife."

The slow movement of her finger stopped. Her eyes dimmed. He kissed her, coaxing a response from her. Her sigh of pleasure heated his blood, his body hardening at the cushion of her breasts and rapid pound of her heart. He lifted her in his arms, carried her down the hall and covered her on their bed.

Logan took his time, touching and tasting her as if he never had before. He kept his eyes open, committing to memory every blush that heated her silky skin, every gasp that parted her lush mouth and every movement that lifted her supple hips. He pressed between her thighs, stilling when her lips parted several times soundlessly.

"What is it?" he urged, brushing her hair from her cheeks and trailing a hand over her breasts.

She hesitated, then shook her head, put a hand around his neck and tugged him close. Her lips parted his, the sweet taste of her filling his mouth and her body wrapping tight around him. He lost himself in her, losing track of where he ended and she began.

Afterward, he held her close until she fell asleep, smoothing a hand over her back and tucking her head beneath his chin as he had every time before. But something was missing. Something that had always been there. The absence of it sent a wave of dread through him.

Logan tightened his arms around Amy, wishing he would hear it. That she would look up at him and say it. But the words never came.

The desperate need weakened him, prompting his heart to pound and his hands to shake against her. He didn't know what scared him the most. The fact that Amy no longer asked him to love her or what he would say if she did.

Chapter Ten

"No, Kayden."

Logan sprang behind the line of large racks housing the New Year's Eve fireworks, scooped Kayden up and tossed him over his shoulder. Kayden squirmed as Logan carried him back across the safe line.

It was almost midnight and so dark Logan couldn't see his hand in front of his nose. Chaotic bursts of laughter, movement and music clamored on the air across the fields beyond them, but the dark night cloaked everything and very little was visible.

"I distinctly remember telling you and your brother to keep your distance." Logan flicked his flashlight upward three times and called out, "Found him, Dom."

The rustle of boots moving over the ground sounded and Dominic stalked out of the darkness surrounding them and into the low lights surrounding the work area. A tall, muscular man ambled up behind him with a pretty redhead at his side.

"I ought to tear your tail up, boy." Dominic blew out a frustrated breath. It hovered on the air in a white puff. "Your aunt Cissy's fit to be tied. You ever run off like that again—"

"Uh-oh," the man at Dominic's side rumbled. "Better take off now, Kayden. Dom's on the warpath."

"Hey, Mr. Colt," Kayden shouted, writhing in an attempt to get down.

Logan laughed and released him, watching as he skipped over and high-fived the man. Colt Mead. One of Dominic's fellow bull riders and playboy extraordinaire.

"Glad you could make it, Colt." Logan shook his hand. "Dom said you might take a break from the circuit and stop in."

"Yeah." Colt ran a broad hand through his blond hair. "Gotta get off the road once in a while or you forget where you are."

"Just as long as you don't stay in one place too long." The redhead nudged Colt with her elbow. "There's a lot of competition out there. You fall behind quick if you don't stay on top of it."

Colt cocked an eyebrow and smiled. "Never met a woman who likes to race as much as Jen does. She might get good at it one day."

"Keep telling yourself that," she said.

Logan chuckled. *Good* was an understatement. From what Colt told him, Jen Taylor was steadily climbing the ranks of barrel racers. She was fast, focused and dedicated. Poised to be at the top of her game if she kept at it.

She traveled with Colt and his cousin, Tammy. The trio was a band of close friends and Logan always enjoyed their visits to Raintree.

Jen smiled. "When there's a break between events, there's no better place to be than Raintree."

"Yep," Colt said. "Even though Dom does his level best to talk me into partnering with him every time I visit. Keeps saying it's time I retire from the circuit and settle down." He chuckled. "I still have plenty of rodeo years left in me, though."

Logan nodded. Next to Dominic, Colt was the most die-hard rider he'd ever met. The man was pure nomad and daredevil. Dom was wasting his time asking him to abandon the rodeo life. Colt wasn't the type of man to stay put anywhere for very long. Or settle down. He enjoyed the circuit—and women—too much.

Kayden tugged on Jen's arms for a kiss and chattered a mile a minute about Santa's recent visit and the approaching fireworks show.

Kayden paused then flashed a hesitant smile. "You can help light the fireworks with me, Ms. Jen."

"Oh, no," Dominic stressed. "You're coming back with me so I can show Aunt Cissy you're still in one piece."

Kayden frowned. "But I want to stay back here and help Uncle Logan with the fireworks."

Logan shook his head. "It's way too dangerous, Kayden. You can see 'em fine from across the field and it's much safer for you over there."

"But Aunt Amy said she's staying," Kayden argued, scrunching his nose.

"Well, there's not much I can do about it." Logan grinned. "She's a hardheaded woman."

"I heard that."

A jaunty bounce of light grew closer and Logan smiled. He flicked his flashlight up and the glow cascaded over Amy's curvy form as she approached. Jayden clasped her hand and skipped along at her side.

"You're in trouble, Uncle Logan." Jayden giggled. "Better say you're sorry."

Logan met them halfway, tapping Jayden's hat and

touching his lips to Amy's ear. "Sorry, babe. But it's true."

Amy harrumphed, her expression playful but strained. Logan knuckled her hat straighter on her head and smoothed a finger over the curve of her cheek, tamping down his frustration.

He'd spent the majority of the week following Christmas coaxing her into bed with him. Her rosy skin glowed, her kisses tasted sweeter than ever and her curves seemed to grow fuller every day. He damn well couldn't get enough of her and every day that passed heightened his anxiety. She still hadn't agreed to stay.

"You must be Amy." Jen reached over the boys and held out a hand. "It's nice to finally meet you."

Pleasantries were exchanged and it wasn't long before Jen was regaling Amy with tales of the barrel racing circuit. Her enthusiasm for the sport was obvious. Colt tensed, shoving his hands in his pockets when Jen described her most recent close call in the arena.

"One of these days, she's not gonna come out of it so lucky," Colt grumbled.

Jen shook her head. "Don't start, Colt. That warning's ironic coming from a bull rider." She smiled at Amy. "*Men.* They're under the mistaken impression that we're the weaker sex."

Amy laughed.

"Fact is," Jen continued, "we all have our dreams. And if they're worth imagining, they're worth chasing." She winked down at the twins. "I'm determined to reach mine."

The boys beamed.

"It's about time to get the show started," Logan said, clapping his hands together.

The boys practically vibrated with excitement and Kayden begged again to stay behind and light the fireworks.

Amy shook her head. "I hate to say it but Logan does have a point." She nudged the twins in Dominic's direction. "It's much safer for you two to watch from the field with everyone else."

The boys groaned in disagreement but darted over to Dominic and pushed at his legs.

"Then let's go so we can get the best seats," Kayden said.

Dominic shook his head. "We had the best seats until you ran off from them."

He smiled and led the boys away. Colt and Jen said their goodbyes and followed, all of them disappearing into the darkness.

Logan waved an arm, signaling to a crew of men to start the proceedings. Scattered shouts from the hands rang out as a couple of the crew moved around, testing and reaffirming everything was in order. Logan took Amy's hand, leading her away from racks of fireworks and farther behind the safety line.

They reached his truck and he released her long enough to rummage inside the cab for another hard hat and set of earplugs.

"Are those really necessary?" Amy asked as he draped the earplugs around her neck.

"Yes." He hooked a finger under her straw hat, swapping it for the hard one. "These aren't backyard firecrackers, Amy. They're extremely dangerous."

She glanced up at the brim of the hard hat. "I guess it'll be worth it." She smiled. "They might be dangerous but you've always put together the most beautiful displays I've ever seen."

"Still do." He smiled. "Wait 'til July rolls around. I'll really impress you then."

His smile slipped. If she was still here.

Amy hesitated, shadows creeping into her eyes. "We need to talk, Logan. About tomorrow."

Logan tensed. The tight note in her voice unsettled him. *Tomorrows.* He'd never been on good terms with them.

She tucked her hair behind her shoulders, fingers trembling slightly. "This was the last day I had on leave from work. I planned on heading back to Augusta first thing tomorrow to start the move."

"But that plan's changed." His chest tightened. "It has changed, hasn't it?"

She stilled, her mouth drawing into a hard line.

"Hey, Logan." Jed waved a flashlight from his stance by the racks of fireworks. "Countdown's about to start. You wanna lead?"

Logan frowned and waved him off. "Nah, you go ahead. You know the drill, yeah?"

Jed nodded and signaled with his flashlight to the rest of the group. They began running final checks for the fireworks show.

"Please tell me you're staying, Amy." Logan's gut churned at her stoic expression. "Things have gone well between us the past few weeks and they can continue that way."

Amy held up a hand. "I want to stay. I really do. But…"

"But, what?" Logan shook his head.

"There's another consideration," she whispered. "A small one."

"What kind of consi—"

"I'm pregnant."

Logan froze. He watched her mouth and waited. Waited for her to take it back. To say she'd misspoken. That it was all a mistake.

A mistake. God help him. *Sara.*

"That's not possible." He bit his lip, a sharp metallic taste seeping onto his tongue. "The doctors said—"

"The doctors said it was highly unlikely." She shook her head, features softening. "Not impossible. We're lucky—"

"*Lucky?*"

"Yes." Her mouth tightened. "We're lucky to have another chance whether we were looking for it or not. Good things can happen just as much as the bad. Life's given us another gift."

Her hand dropped to cover her belly. His gut churned and he swallowed hard, looking away.

Sporadic yellow lights flickered over the ground as the hands moved about with flashlights on the other side of the lot, checking the racks and getting into final positions.

"How long have you known?" His voice sounded strange, even to his own ears.

"It was confirmed a couple of days ago. I didn't want to mention it until I knew for sure." Her tone gentled. "I'm sure now."

Sure. Logan's mouth twisted. She'd been sure when she'd gotten pregnant with Sara. Had been sure their daughter was okay even when he'd insisted something was wrong. Sure they'd deliver a healthy baby girl.

Logan shoved his hands in his pockets and moved away. There was no such thing as being sure. Nothing was ever certain. Not for this pregnancy and not for Amy.

What if...

"We can't go through this again," he choked. "What happens when we lose this baby? You think it'll hurt any less than before?"

"I want this child." Amy squared her shoulders. "I was told that as long as I'm careful, things may work out. There's a chance nothing will go wrong this time."

"As much chance as there was the first time? With Sara?" His voice cracked, his throat tightening to the point of pain. "What about her? She was once part of our family, too. Have you forgotten her?"

She winced, whispering, "I've never forgotten Sara. Not for one day. And I never will." Her chin lifted. "But nothing you or I did caused us to lose her. It just happened. I won't let the pain of losing Sara stop me from living." She touched his arm. "Life goes on, Logan."

He flinched, pulling away. *"It shouldn't."*

A searing heat washed through his chest, flooding it as though his heart was bleeding out.

The shaking in his hands was becoming a violent tremor. "What if something happens to you? I just got you back."

"You've never had me," she said. "Not really."

"You're my *wife*."

Amy's smile was sad. "That's just a word, Logan. One you throw out to excuse the lie I told. What you use to console yourself every time you give in to me. Something you say to feel honorable for keeping your promise and sticking it out." She shook her head. "I'm not your wife. I'm just an obligation. Another one of your regrets."

Pain swept over Logan, leaving him hollow and weak.

"That's not true," he said.

A voice boomed over the loudspeaker, signaling the start of the New Year's Eve countdown. Portfires burst into bright red flames across the lot as the men approached the fuses. The crowd, hidden in the darkness, cheered and the chant began.

Ten. Nine...

"That's not true," he repeated.

Seven. Six...

She blinked, her wide green eyes lifting and meeting his.

Four. Three...

"I can make this work, Amy."

One. Happy New Year!

A massive round of explosions cracked through the air. The black sky burst into color with scattered streaks of light. The boom from the firecrackers echoed through the ground beneath their feet, smoke and ash scattering all around them.

Amy cringed, the green light from above casting an eerie glow over her. Logan pressed his hands over her ears and held her close as the pyrotechnics continued, the explosions sounding closer together and growing louder.

The fireworks stopped. The cheers of the crowd took over and smoke billowed in big, dark clouds around them.

"I can make this right," he rasped.

Amy yanked at his wrists, pulling his hands from her

ears. "There's no wrong to be made right. This pregnancy will not be another obligation. This baby and I deserve to be loved."

"*Loved?*" Logan shook his head. "You don't know what that means—"

"Yes, I do. You're the one who doesn't know what real love is. Everything you offer comes with conditions and expectations. You only accept people when they live up to your standards and can't forgive them when they don't." Her fingers wove into his hair and rubbed over his nape. "You have to believe love exists to be able to feel it. My love isn't enough for you and your loyalty isn't enough for me. Neither of us can win. It's time for us to go our separate ways."

His legs grew weak. "You can't go through this pregnancy alone."

"Yes, I can," she said. "I'd rather be alone than with someone who could never truly love me for who I am."

Amy took the hard hat off her head, slid the earplugs from her neck and held them out. Logan took them.

"This pregnancy might not work out," she said. "I might lose this baby like we lost Sara. It may even hurt worse than it did before." She hesitated, looking away. "Or, things could turn out differently. I might end up with a healthy child and be happier than I ever thought possible." She faced him again, her small smile determined. "Maybe I'm a dreamer. Maybe I am still chasing a fairy tale. But I'm not giving up on it. No matter what happens, I don't want to just exist. I want to live."

She grabbed her hat from the truck and left, her long strides taking her farther and farther away. Logan balled his fists and tried to take a step. Tried to follow. But he couldn't. His heart, heavy with pain and regret, rooted him to the ground.

Cheerful shouts from the crowd echoed over the field and the rhythmic pound of music drifted on the night air. The smoke cleared and the stars shone brighter than ever.

Logan stood alone again, stuck between the present and the past, waiting for Amy to return. And watching life move on without him.

FIVE O'CLOCK. AMY TUCKED her watch beneath the sleeve of her sweater and raised her head, looking out at the dark fields before her. The glowing hands on her wristwatch haunted her vision and floated in bright smudges across the landscape on the other side of the porch rail.

She rocked back in her chair and sighed. New Year's Eve had officially ended and she'd spent the first five hours of New Year's Day rocking on a porch, staring into the darkness and waiting. Something she'd never been any good at, even under the best of circumstances. And Logan had still not returned to the main house.

She'd known the news of the pregnancy would be hard for him. Had expected it to unsettle him. But she'd also hoped he'd seek her out after recovering from the shock. That she'd have an opportunity to say goodbye on better terms and reassure him that he'd always be welcome in their child's life.

Only, Logan hadn't sought her out. The one glimpse she'd had of him since the fireworks show had been his moonlit figure as he'd entered the stable then left with Lightning.

The screen door creaked open. A tall figure emerged

onto the porch, taking long strides toward the line of rocking chairs and halting abruptly in front of hers.

"Damn, kid," Dominic boomed. "You crackin' dawn in for everyone or what?"

Amy smiled despite her ill mood. "Is that how you say good morning these days?"

Dominic chuckled, plopping down in the chair beside her and cradling a cup in his hands. "Good morning." He tipped his cup at her, the pleasant aroma of coffee rising with each curl of steam. "You want? Your mama just brewed a fresh pot. It'll help wake you up."

She shook her head. "I've been up."

"Couldn't sleep?"

"Didn't want to." She forced a half smile. "I've slept more than my fair share over the last four years."

Dominic's grin slipped. "I won't argue with you there. It's good to have you back." He sipped from his mug, glancing out at the horizon and rocking. The wood chair creaked with each of his movements. "Sun's comin' up soon. That what you've been out here waiting on?"

"No. I've been waiting for you." Which had become true at some point in the wee hours, when she'd given up on Logan returning…

He smiled, his expression tinged with amusement. "'Course you have." He propped his boots on the porch rail. "I'm always in high demand."

Amy laughed and smacked his arm. Dominic's wise-cracks alone were enough to clear the grit from her eyes and lift her spirits.

"I was hoping you'd drive me to Augusta today," she said. "It seems I've lost my ride."

He frowned. "You're still leaving?"

She nodded.

"Why?" At her silence, Dominic added, "I thought you and Logan were getting along better lately."

"I'm pregnant."

His boots dropped from the rail with a thud. "Well. I guess y'all are getting along *a lot* better lately."

Amy swallowed hard, vision blurring. "Not anymore."

Dominic stilled. "He didn't take it well?"

Hot tears scalded her cheeks, rolling slowly down her face and dripping off her chin. "No."

"Ah, hell, Ames." Dominic set his cup on the porch rail with a thunk and crouched at her side, wrapping her hands in his. "I hate that that happened. But he's had a hard time coming to terms with losing Sara. Give him some room. A little time to adjust—"

"That's something I can't give him." She tugged her hands free and scrubbed them across her face. "We've lost too much time already. Both of us."

"So you're gonna leave? Just like that?" Dominic shook his head. "That'll kill him, Amy."

She sighed and rocked back in the chair. "No. Losing Sara already did that. When Logan looks at me, all he sees is the past. We've both spent enough time there. I have to move on for this baby, and maybe if the reminder's gone, he'll finally move on, too."

"I can't help you do this." He stood and took a step back. "I can't do this to Logan."

"It's the only thing I *can* do. I already love this baby as much as I loved Sara. This child deserves a fair shot at life and all my support to thrive. I can't provide that buried underneath Logan's guilt and regret." She raised a hand in appeal. "Logan doesn't love me. I've faced that. Come to terms with it. And I won't stay here just to be tolerated."

Dominic turned away, but didn't immediately leave.

She straightened. "It's time for me to move on, Dom. I'm leaving. With or without your help. But I'd be lying if I said I didn't need it. I could really use a friend right now."

He slowly turned back to face her. His frown dissolved and a tight smile took its place. "How soon do you want to head out?"

Amy finished packing within an hour, throwing in everything she'd brought with her except for two items she decided to leave behind. She slipped the necklace over her head and dropped the ring onto the papers on the dresser, swapping them out for her black straw hat.

She took her bags to the kitchen, hugged Pop and Cissy and said the rest of her goodbyes in the driveway while Dominic loaded her luggage in the truck.

"Remember you're loved," Betty whispered, hugging her tighter. "No matter where you are."

Traci wiped away tears and tried to smile. "I want first-class tickets, sis. Not crappy economy."

It was hard saying goodbye to Betty and Traci but it was sheer torture walking away from the boys.

"But who's gonna take care of Thunder and keep him happy?" Jayden looked down and twisted the toe of his shoe in the dirt, his cowboy hat hiding his face.

"I was hoping you and Kayden could do that for me. And maybe look out for your uncle Logan, too?" Amy glanced at Kayden and he nodded with a brave smile.

"We can do it, Aunt Amy." Kayden elbowed his brother, mouth quivering. "Can't we, Jayden?"

"Yeah," Jayden whispered. His wide blue eyes peeked

up at her from beneath the brim of his hat, glistening with tears. "But who'll keep you happy? You won't have Thunder no more. And you won't have us."

Amy's heart squeezed. She knelt down and hugged the boys close. "Oh, I'll always have the two of you, baby. I'm carrying you both with me." She leaned back and placed a hand over her heart. "Right here."

With Sara. And with Logan... She smiled, blinking back her own tears and forcing down the lump in her throat.

"Just like you both will have me." She touched her hands to their chests. "Right here."

Kayden rubbed his eyes with his fists. "Will you come back and visit?"

"Of course," she said. "And your aunt Cissy and I already talked about you coming to see me in Michigan. Maybe next Christmas?"

She felt excitement stirring at the hope of holding her own child on Christmas morning. She straightened Kayden's hat and squeezed his arms.

"There's real snow up there," she said. "You and Jayden can make huge snowballs and throw as many as you want. It won't hurt like the ice."

Jayden perked up. "Real snow? Lots of it?"

"Mountains of it. As far as the eye can see."

Grins broke out across their faces.

Amy kissed the twins once more, hugged Cissy and waited in the truck while Dominic assured Cissy one last time that he'd return safely, soon. He hopped in and they strapped on their seat belts.

Amy glanced up at the sunlight beaming through the windshield. She noticed Logan then. He was several yards away, sitting astride Lightning in the center of the adjoining field. His Stetson was pulled down low and he remained motionless, watching them.

"He's hurtin', Amy," Dominic murmured. "As much as you were."

"I know." She twisted her hands together in her lap, resisting the urge to fling the door open and run straight to him.

"You sure you wanna leave?"

"No." Amy tore her eyes away from Logan, straightened and faced the road ahead. "But I'm done standing still."

Dominic nodded, cranked the truck and drove away.

Chapter Eleven

Divorce Settlement Agreement.

Logan smoothed his fingertips over the words. The papers crinkled under his touch, the edges worn. He bent them in half then folded them over. Once, twice then a third time, and returned the bundle to the dresser.

The action had become a habit over the past week. One he'd undertaken every night before crawling into an empty bed and every morning when he finally gave up chasing sleep to face the day.

The day. God help him. The things kept coming. Rolling in with the sun, spanning what seemed like thousands of hours and hanging on through the darkness. A darkness he failed to find relief in.

He ached for Amy. His chest burned for her and his hands turned numb from clenching empty air every time he reached for her in the night. Every part of him wanted to follow her but the heavy weight in his chest held him hostage where he stood.

Logan sighed and dragged a hand over his face. Every day, he tried to make himself go and bring Amy back. And, every day, he failed.

"Uncle Logan?"

He spun from the dresser to find the boys hovering in

the bedroom doorway. Jayden picked at the legs of his jeans and Kayden peeked up at him with a concerned expression. The same one he'd worn every afternoon for the past week as he'd followed him close, at Logan's heels around the ranch after school.

"Hey." Logan cleared the husky note from his voice and strived for a cheerful tone. "You two are up early for a Sunday."

Jayden nodded, hands clutching his hat in front of his waist. "We asked Uncle Dominic to get us up. We wanna help you with the horses today."

"You sure you want to spend your day off school working? It'll be a long one."

"Yes, sir," Kayden said.

Jayden put his hat on his head, straightening the brim with both hands, and stuck out his chest. "We promised Aunt Amy we'd take care of Thunder for her." He tried for a smile but it drooped at the corners. "So, can we help?"

Logan nodded. "There's nothing I'd like more."

He crossed the room and held out his hands. They latched on to them and they took their time making their way to the stables, just as they had every afternoon over the past week.

Winter was in full swing and this morning was no exception. The January air whipped through their clothes with cold gusts of wind as they strolled down the winding path, flushing Kayden's cheeks and making Jayden shiver. Logan stopped, bending to fasten the top button on their jean jackets and tug their hats down firmer around their ears.

"We're all right." Jayden batted his hands away and strutted on with his brother.

"Yeah," Kayden said. "We don't get cold no more."

"Oh, yeah?" Logan's mouth twitched. "Why's that?"

Kayden jerked his chin. "'Cuz we're bone-a-fine cowboys now. Mr. Jed said they don't never get cold."

Logan clamped his lips shut, choking back his laughter. It was probably best to let that one go. Wouldn't do for him to question Mr. Jed's knowledge. The boys didn't take too kindly to others criticizing the ranch hand's words of wisdom.

They spent the first couple hours of the morning turning horses out and mucking stalls alongside the hands. When the twins' shoulders began to sag, Logan took the shovels from them and suggested a break. He led them outside and lifted them to the top rail of the white fence lining the paddock, keeping an arm snug around each of the boys' backs.

"We got a treat for Thunder." Jayden dug around in his pocket then drew out a small, colorful lump. "It's oats and carrots and the sugar stuff mixed together."

"Yeah," Kayden said. "Ms. Betty helped us make it last night."

Logan held Jayden's palm and tilted it from one side to the other. No sign of cayenne powder this time.

He smiled. "I think he'll enjoy that. Hold it out and let him have a taste."

Logan clucked his tongue and steadied Jayden's outstretched arm as Thunder walked over. The stallion moved gracefully, his muscles rippling. Thunder nudged Jayden's hand with his nose then wrapped his lips around the treat and nibbled.

Kayden giggled. "He likes it."

Thunder's soft breaths and chomping teeth filled the silence that followed until the treat disappeared. The stallion licked Jayden's palm, setting off another round of laughter from the boys, then turned and strolled away.

Kayden tilted his head back, glancing up at him. "Uncle Dominic said you're the best trainer there is. 'Cept for Aunt Amy." He blinked and lifted his chin. "I ain't scared of Thunder no more, and I can learn to ride him like Aunt Amy does. You think you could teach me one day?"

"One day. But not quite yet. Thunder might be having more good days than bad, but he's still adjusting."

Jayden pursed his lips. "Bet he misses Aunt Amy."

Logan's gut churned. He looked away, focusing on the other horses milling about in the field. "I expect so."

Kayden sighed and picked at Logan's sleeve. "We miss her, too."

Logan tightened his arms around the boys, tugging them closer and whispering, "So do I."

The twins huddled into Logan's chest and wrapped their arms around his back. They stayed silent for a while, gazing across the fields and listening to the gentle sounds of the horses.

A breathless cry and pounding feet shattered the silence.

"It's time!"

Logan glanced over his shoulder. Traci loped down the path from the main house. She stopped, bending with her hands on her knees and struggling to drag in air.

"Time for what?" Jayden asked, squirming against Logan's chest.

"Time…" Traci gulped and grinned "…for the babies." She straightened and pointed to the main house. "Mama and Pop just left for the hospital with Dom and

Cissy. Mama said to come get you so you could drive the rest of us."

Traci darted back up the path, flapping her hands and sputtering over her shoulder, "Well, come on."

Logan made short order of loading Traci and the boys into the truck and took off for the hospital as fast as safety allowed. The drive seemed to take longer than usual and Logan's hands shook harder against the steering wheel with every giddy exclamation from Traci.

"I can't wait to see Grace and Gwen," she gushed, biting her lip and bouncing in the passenger seat. "Bet they'll be beautiful."

"Yeah," Kayden drawled, kicking the back of her seat, "'til they start cryin' and poopin'. Mr. Jed said that's all babies do."

"Hush up, squirt." Traci glanced in the rearview mirror and narrowed her eyes. "Mr. Jed's full of hot air. You oughta be glad you're getting cousins."

Kayden wasn't impressed. He curled his lip and turned to stare out of the window, remaining quiet for the rest of the journey.

The waiting room was crowded, and they filled up the last row of empty chairs by the window. Pop and Betty walked around the corner, a smile wreathing both their faces.

"Everything's well underway," Pop said. "The doc told us things are moving fast. So it shouldn't be long now."

"Dominic's a nervous wreck." Betty laughed. "Good thing it'll be over with soon."

Logan shifted in his seat and hoped that was the case. He ran his eyes over the others in the waiting room. Fathers, siblings and grandparents all moved with excited energy around the chairs. They tapped their toes, flashed nervous grins and sprang up for hugs at the delivery of good news.

This continued throughout the course of the morning, carrying over into late afternoon. For the other families. There was, however, no happy word on Dominic and Cissy, and the silence stretched into late evening.

Logan shoved to his feet and paced the waiting room. His legs tingled, blood rushing back in and tight muscles stretching.

Traci's knees bounced with jerky movements and Betty wrung her hands in her lap. The twins hunched in their chairs, hats shielding their expressions. Pop left for the third time in the past hour to check for more news.

"You boys want to run down to the cafeteria and grab something to eat?" Betty smiled and crouched in front of the boys.

They shook their heads.

"Are you sure?" Betty asked. "It's been a long time since y'all had breakfast and you didn't have any lunch or supper."

"I'm not hungry," Jayden mumbled.

"I wanna wait for Aunt Cissy." Kayden's hat tipped up as he looked around the room. "Lots of other people got their babies already." His voice shook. "Why ain't ours here yet?"

"I don't know," Betty said gently. "But they'll get here eventually. Sometimes, it takes a while." She glanced up and stood. "Here comes your uncle Dominic now. Maybe he'll have some good news for us."

Or maybe not. Logan's stomach dropped as he watched his brother stride swiftly across the room. His hair stood up at odd angles and his face was shadowed. Pop followed a step behind with the same grim expression.

The boys ran to Dominic and he squatted, drawing them both between his knees, squeezing their arms and kissing the tops of their heads.

"Are the babies here yet?" Kayden asked.

Dominic's throat moved on a hard swallow. "Gwen is." A smile flitted across his lips. "She's got dark hair—" he tapped their noses "—but her eyes are as blue as yours."

"What about the other one?" Jayden asked.

Dominic stood and nudged the boys toward Betty. "Grace will be here soon, too. Now, go sit with Traci and I'll come get you when it's time."

"Come on, boys," Pop said. He took their hands and led them over to join Traci.

Logan stepped close, eyeing the worried glint in Dominic's eyes. "What's going on?"

"Grace—" Dominic's voice cracked. He bit his lip and looked away. "Grace is showing signs of distress. They said the cord prolapsed and she's not getting enough oxygen so they took Cissy for an emergency C-section. If they don't make it to Grace in time..."

"Oh, Dom." Betty patted Dominic's arm. "You hang in there. There are good doctors taking care of your girls."

Dominic nodded, his gaze moving over her shoulder. Kayden scrambled into Traci's lap. She hugged him close and surveyed Dominic with a worried expression.

"Cissy asked me to check on the boys," Dominic said. "She wanted me to let them know everything was gonna be okay."

"We'll take care of them," Betty said, moving away

to drop a kiss to the twins' foreheads. "You tell her not to worry."

Dominic stood, watching the boys, shoulders sagging and mouth twisting. Logan's throat closed.

"I've got to get back." Dominic pressed his thumb and forefinger to his closed eyelids and dropped his head. "Cissy's exhausted and worried sick about Grace. I've never seen her this terrified." He looked up, eyes hovering on Logan's, and whispered, "And there's not a thing I can do to help either one of them."

Logan froze. Sara was on Dominic's mind. It was right there in every defeated line of his brother's body. And seeing that kind of pain hanging on Dominic burned in his chest.

He gripped Dominic's shoulder and squeezed, forcing sound out of his constricted throat. "Cissy's strong. She's gonna pull through this. And if Grace inherited even half of the grit you and Cissy have, she'll come out either smiling or swinging a fist."

There was no way to tell how much truth was in the words. The outcome would remain uncertain to the last second, no matter what anyone said. But it comforted Dominic and that was all that mattered.

Dominic nodded. "Cissy *is* strong. The strongest woman I've ever met." He managed a small smile. "Aside from Amy."

Dominic strode across the room toward the hall but stopped, turned back and said, "I'm glad I came home. Glad Cissy and I settled at Raintree. Don't think we could make it through this without all of you." He smiled, the fear in his eyes still present but determination overcoming it. "Having people you love around makes you stronger. No matter how tough it gets."

Logan watched him leave. He'd never seen Dominic stand so tall or move with such strength. In that one moment, Logan was the proudest he'd ever been of his little brother.

Logan returned to his chair. Jayden leaned onto the arm of it, staring down at his boots and frowning.

"Hey," Logan said, "wanna sit with me for a while?"

Jayden nodded, his blond curls slipping onto his forehead. Logan sat down and settled him in his lap. He caught sight of Jayden's hat lying upside down on the floor.

"Did you lose your hat?" Logan reached for it.

"No." Jayden stilled him with a hand on his forearm. "I just ain't no bone-a-fine cowboy no more."

"Why not?"

Jayden glanced up, blue eyes blurred with tears. "'Cuz I'm scared."

"For your aunt Cissy and Grace?"

Jayden nodded. "Mr. Jed said bone-a-fine cowboys are always brave. That they don't never get scared."

Logan winced. He knew the weight of that worry. The need to be strong. The need to always be perfect and never make a mistake. Otherwise, what would there be for anyone to respect? To admire? To love?

Love. He tensed, Amy's words returning.

Everything you offer comes with conditions and expectations.

Logan tipped Jayden's chin up with a knuckle and peered into his eyes. "It's okay to be afraid. Most everyone is at some point or another. It's pushing through the fear that makes you brave."

Jayden blinked and asked, "So I can still be a bone-a-fine cowboy?"

Logan nodded. "Yep. And a bone-a-fine cowboy always looks better wearing a hat." He scooped it off the floor and placed it on Jayden's head. "A man needs his hat."

Jayden brightened, a smile stretching from ear to ear. He snuggled against the left side of Logan's chest—Amy's favorite spot—settling in for the long wait.

You only accept people when they live up to your standards and can't forgive them when they don't.

Logan cringed. He'd never lived up to his own standards. Had never pleased himself with his own actions, much less been impressed by anyone else's. He'd been so fixated on flawlessness that he'd failed to see the good qualities in others.

Dominic had left the circuit for Cissy. Not because he had to but because he wanted to. For her and the boys.

Even though it'd almost broken him, Pop had stayed behind at Raintree instead of following Gloria. Not because he hadn't still loved her but because he loved his sons more.

Amy had held the memory of their marriage in her heart for four years. Had remained loyal to it and to him. Not because she had to. But because she loved him.

You have to believe love exists to be able to feel it.

He *had* felt it. Every time he held Amy, hands shaking against her. Every time his body rebelled against his mind, reaching for her and getting lost in her over and over again. And he'd felt it burning in his chest when he'd held Sara.

He'd fought feeling it to avoid pain and regret. To avoid the risk of losing Amy and being hurt. Turned out, his heart was stronger than his head. It had remained steadfast to Amy through the worst.

I'm just an obligation. Another one of your regrets.

He didn't want Amy because of a piece of paper. Or to make up for any mistakes they made. He wanted her because he needed her. He needed her spirit and smile in his life. Needed her hardheaded stubbornness and tender touch. Needed her because she challenged him and made him feel more alive than anything else. The love he had for her was stronger and more comforting than any pain life's disappointments could bring.

Logan's throat thickened. He'd never told her he loved her. Not once. Hell, he hadn't even been able to acknowledge it to himself.

The next few minutes ticked by in slow motion. One hour passed and then another. The boys' eyes drooped but they stayed awake, Kayden in Traci's lap and Jayden in Logan's. Pop paced and Betty wiped tears away a time or two.

Dominic burst into the waiting room, his smile as wide as his step. "Cissy's doing well. They moved her into a room. Get over here, boys. You have an aunt asking for you and two cousins to visit."

"So Grace is okay?" Pop's smile shook.

Dominic hugged him. "Yeah. She's perfect. All my girls are."

Relief flooded Logan's chest. The boys squealed and hopped to the floor, clamoring across the room to barrel into Dominic's legs. They each looped an arm around his thighs and stood on his boots, laughing as his strides carried them down the hall.

"Well—" Dominic's brow quirked "—y'all waiting for an engraved invitation, or what?"

They all laughed and followed Dominic. Logan stayed back, waiting in the hall as Betty and Traci cooed over the girls. Pop's deep voice sounded as he spoke in soothing tones to Cissy and the babies and the boys' proud chatter filled every corner of the room. Everyone was there.

Everyone except Amy. Logan closed his eyes. He wanted a new life with her and their baby. Wanted to hope again for the dream he'd lost so long ago with Sara.

Maybe I am still chasing a fairy tale. But I'm not giving up on it.

Amy's words warmed his blood and lifted his head. He opened his eyes, excitement buzzing in his veins at the possibility. The hope of happiness. Of something bright and beautiful growing out of something that was once so bleak.

"We're heading back now," Pop said, stepping into the hall. "Dom's spending the night here. You coming?"

Logan shook his head. "I'm gonna stay with Dom for a while. Can the boys and Traci ride back with you and Betty? It's late and I don't know how long I'll be."

Pop smiled. "Of course. Take your time."

Betty and Traci passed, discussing plans for the new twins' wardrobe. Kayden and Jayden smacked noisy kisses to Cissy's cheeks, then skipped into the hall.

"What'd you think?" Logan asked.

Kayden tilted his head and shrugged. "They ain't bad. Kinda small but they're okay, I guess."

"We like 'em," Jayden said. "We're gonna take good care of 'em."

"I know you will." Logan swept them against his legs for a squeeze before they scampered off to join the rest of the crew walking down the hall.

Logan inhaled, holding his breath and edging his head into the room. Dominic sat at Cissy's bedside. He smoothed one hand over her blond hair and the other over the babies nestled in her arms.

Logan cleared his throat and asked, "Got time for one more visitor?"

They glanced up and smiled.

"Of course," Cissy said. "Come meet your nieces."

Logan walked slowly to the bed. "You feeling okay?"

Cissy laughed. "I'm feeling great right now. It's tomorrow when the meds wear off that things will change."

Logan nodded and looked at the bundles in her arms. The boys had been right. The babies were small. The pink blankets cocooning them parted slightly to reveal dark hair, flushed cheeks and rosebud mouths. Every bit of which reminded him of Sara.

Logan flinched, pain shooting through his chest. Not as sharp as before but enough to cut.

"They're beautiful, aren't they?" Dominic bent and kissed their foreheads.

Logan nodded and searched their peaceful faces, waiting for their eyelids to flicker or their mouths to part.

"Would you like to hold one of them?" Cissy asked.

Her eyes were patient and gentle. Understanding.

Logan swallowed around the lump in his throat. "Please."

Dominic stood and Logan took his seat, watching with coiled muscles as Dominic gently lifted one of the babies and carried her over.

"Here you go, Grace," Dominic whispered, lowering her into Logan's arms. "Meet your uncle Logan."

Grace's light weight hardly rivaled a feather and if he didn't have his eyes on her, Logan could've sworn

Dominic had never put her in his arms. He held still and studied her face. She didn't move. Didn't make a sound.

Sara.

Logan froze. A knot formed in his chest. He pulled Grace closer.

"There's something wrong."

Heaven help him, he knew the thought was irrational. Knew it to be untrue. But he couldn't stop himself from voicing it.

"No," Cissy whispered. "She's just sleeping."

Logan shook his head. His eyes burned. The dark, downy head blurred in front of him, the delicate features distorting.

"She's not breathing—" Tremors stole his voice and racked his body as he studied her chest.

"Yes, she is." Cissy's hand touched his forearm.

He tore his eyes away from Grace and focused on Cissy's face.

Cissy smiled. "She's perfectly fi—"

A cry pierced the air, cracking the stillness and echoing around the room. They all started. Logan curled his hands around the bundle, the warmth of her seeping into his palms.

"Here." Dominic reached out, his face shadowed with concern. "I think Grace is gonna turn out to be the fussy one. You can hold Gwen."

"Wait, Dominic."

Logan barely registered Cissy's words. Grace demanded his attention. Her face scrunched up and an angry flush engulfed her cheeks. That small mouth parted and the biggest, shrillest cry he'd ever heard broke free, causing Dominic to cringe and provoking wails from Gwen.

Something cracked wide open in Logan's chest and every heavy pain he harbored came rushing out. Tears poured from his eyes in scalding streaks and rattled free of his body with each shudder ripping through his limbs.

His chest shook then. It jerked with strong bursts of laughter and he blinked away the tears to smile down at the howling bundle in his arms.

"Cry, baby girl. You cry all you want. Let the whole damn world know you're in it."

Grace opened her eyes. Those beautiful blues widened up at him, her cries fading away. She blinked and took up squirming, the pink blanket shifting with each thrust of her legs and arms. One tiny fist broke free and made its way to her mouth. Her lips moved with sucking sounds and she frowned. The fist flailed and Grace released a more demanding cry.

Logan looked up, returning Cissy and Dominic's smiles with one of his own. "You were right, Dom. She's perfect."

For once, Logan's arms were heavier than his heart.

Logan made it back to the ranch in record time. He refused to wait for the sun to rise. Instead, he threw essentials into his overnight bag, grabbed the packet of papers and ring then stuffed them into his pocket.

He hopped into his truck, twisted the key in the ignition and slammed his foot on the pedal. He could just make out Raintree's main house in the rearview mirror as he drove away, the taillights casting a red glow through the haze of dust billowing up behind him.

Logan smiled. It still hurt to look back but it felt good to move forward.

"DO YOU NEED another box? There's more in the break room."

Amy puffed a strand of hair out of her face and stretched a strip of packing tape across the top of the box in her office chair. She glanced up, smiling at the receptionist hovering in the doorway.

"No, thanks, Kimberly. I think this will do it."

Amy smoothed a hand over the tape, then sighed with satisfaction. It had taken several days to finish packing up everything at her apartment and her office but the task had been a welcome distraction since she'd left Raintree. Everything was taped up and ready to go. Except for her heart.

"You'll be missed around here." Kimberly sighed, studying the two boxes stacked on top of the mahogany desk. "I sure hope the newbie coming in knows their stuff."

Amy laughed. "I imagine that's what someone is saying about me right now in Michigan."

"Maybe so. But I've really enjoyed working with you. I know this is a good opportunity but I wish you didn't have to go."

Amy's smile slipped. She'd wished the same thing over the past week. Wished she didn't have to leave Raintree's sprawling fields or her family. She missed Betty's cooking, Pop's bear hugs, Traci's good-natured banter with the boys, Dom, Cissy and...*Logan*. She missed Logan so much more than she ever had. She wished she could go back to Raintree for good. Wished—

"I wish I didn't have to go, either," Amy said, straightening her shoulders. "But sometimes, you have to move on whether you want to or not. Take the bad right along with the good."

Kimberly nodded, calling over her shoulder as she left, "I'll be right out front if you need anything."

Amy closed her eyes, unable to stop herself from wishing one last time that things were different. That this move would be to Raintree instead of in the other direction. That Logan would be at her side, hoping for the best for this baby and making their family complete.

She placed a hand over her belly and focused on the good. *Six weeks.* New life had thrived within her for six weeks. A life she and Logan had created.

Today was difficult. Driving to the airport in the morning would be even worse. But the next day would be better. So would the next. Eventually, more good days would come. And she'd appreciate them more than ever before because she had known the bad. Of that, she was certain.

Amy smiled and lifted the last box from the chair, setting it on top of the desk with the others. A heavy tread sounded down the hallway followed by the rapid click of Kimberly's heels.

"Sir, please." Kimberly's breathless voice echoed in from the hall. "Wait one minute so I—"

"I'm through waiting."

Amy's head shot up at the low words. Logan strode into the room, closed the door and rounded the desk. She caught a glimpse of the determined set of his jaw and warm, dark eyes before he claimed her mouth.

His lips parted hers, the familiar taste and masculine scent of him overwhelming her. The heat of his touch spread from her shoulders down her back and over her bottom, his broad palms kneading and caressing along the way. The tender advance continued, Logan's touch faltering when a soft cry escaped her.

His hands stilled on her waist. He lifted his head, nuzzled his cheek against hers and whispered in her ear, "Just so we're clear, babe, that wasn't for practice."

Her heart flipped over at his gentle grin. "I don't think you need any."

"Ask me."

She blinked. "Ask you what?"

"Ask me why I wanted you to stay."

Amy hesitated, belly fluttering. "Wh-why did you want me to stay?"

His big palms cradled her face, thumbs sweeping over her cheeks. "Because I love you, Amy. Always have in one way or another. I was so afraid of things not working out that I didn't trust it. Didn't want to risk losing you or make a mistake. And, after losing Sara, I didn't want to take a chance on anything. But I want to now. I want to move forward. With you."

He kissed her again, each sweep of his tongue and glide of his hands making her knees weaker. A low moan escaped his lips and entered her mouth.

She trembled, leaning back and trying to catch her breath. "Say it again."

He smiled. "I love you," he repeated. "Always have. Always will."

"I love you, too, Logan."

He brushed his hand through her hair, dark eyes locking with hers. "Thank God for that." His palm slid around her waist to cover her belly. "I'm ready. For everything. Anything. No matter what happens."

"Does that mean you're here to bring me home?"

"No. You're my home. Wherever you go, I follow."

He stepped back and pulled the pack of divorce papers from his pocket. His tanned hands held them up and ripped them several times over. The torn pieces fluttered to the floor in a soft, white shower of chaotic disarray.

"I want to start over." He took her hand, slipped her ring on her finger and ran his fingertip over the band. "Live every day of my life to the fullest, with you in it."

She fought to ignore the heated rush of her blood and studied his face. "Things may not work out any better with this pregnancy than they did before."

"Or they might." He slid his hands over her hips and pressed a kiss to her forehead. "Whatever happens, we'll pull through it. The good and the bad because we're stronger together." His expression softened. "We'll make our own fairy tale."

He kissed her again, his mouth tasting and teasing. Amy wrapped her arms around his neck and returned his kiss, holding him tighter.

Her rapid breaths mingled with his. "Let's start home."

"To Raintree?" He brightened at her nod, a wide smile stretching across his lean cheeks. "Are you sure?"

Amy kissed him again, whispering against his lips, "Everything I love is there. There's no place in the world I'd rather be."

Epilogue

Hope. One syllable with so much promise and the richest reward. The most comforting word in existence.

Logan smiled and spun the crib mobile with his fingertips. The silver stars dangling from the center glinted in the low light of the bedroom lamp with each twist. His son's eyes followed the movement, wide with wonder.

"Give it a try, Ethan," he whispered.

Ethan curled his knees to his chest and kicked his feet against the mattress. His gaze refocused on the star above and he stretched his arms up. At four months old, he had difficulty controlling the direction of his movements but he gave it his best shot anyway. His small hands opened and closed, his fingers dancing in the air as he tried to capture the shiny object.

"You can do it." Logan held out his finger, raising it just beyond his son's reach.

Ethan shifted his attention to Logan's hand and his grasping fingers followed. He caught hold of Logan's finger, wrapping it tight in his palm. His eyebrows lifted and a smile broke out across his face as he gurgled with delight.

Logan chuckled. "That's my boy."

"Are you two still playing?"

Slim arms encircled Logan from behind, hands splaying over his chest and soft curves pressing against his back. His body tightened, flooding with warmth. He turned, wrapping his hands around Amy's hips and tugging her close.

"Feeling left out?" he teased, touching a kiss to her nose. "Because I'd be more than happy to schedule extra playtime for us if that'd raise your spirits."

"Hmm. That might be a good idea…"

Her head tilted back as he kissed her neck. He moved his mouth over her skin, breathing in her sweet scent and touching the tip of his tongue to the pulse at the base of her throat.

He closed his eyes, savoring the taste and feel of her, and knew he'd never get enough. His love for Amy grew every day and this one was no exception. They'd had an extra busy Christmas morning with family, followed by a boisterous afternoon playing with the kids, and they should all be exhausted. But it seemed none of them were ready to call it a night.

A disgruntled cry emerged from the crib. Logan groaned, stealing one more kiss as Amy edged around him.

"What's the matter, handsome?" Amy slipped her hands under Ethan and lifted him to her chest, murmuring soothing words.

Logan grinned and stroked his palm over Ethan's downy black hair. "We've gotta work on your timing, son."

"Oh, he'll settle down soon." Amy kissed the top of Ethan's head and rubbed a hand over his back. "He just likes a stroll before bedtime."

She crossed the bedroom and stood by the window, humming a Christmas tune and swaying from side to side. Ethan's eyes grew heavy and eventually fluttered shut, his rosy cheek pressed tight to Amy's chest.

A wave of sweet heat rushed through Logan. Dear God, they were beautiful. The most precious parts of his life.

"Logan." Amy glanced over her shoulder, mouth parting with excitement. "Come look."

He moved close, wrapping his arms around them both and looking out the window. The glow of the white Christmas lights lining the porch rails of the house spilled over, illuminating the space below their window. A silent shower of puffy white flakes fluttered to the ground. They piled up to form a festive blanket that tucked up against the edge of the house.

"A white Christmas." She laughed softly. "In Georgia. Can you believe it?"

"Yeah." Logan squeezed Amy closer and smoothed a palm over his son's back. "Anything is possible."

They stayed awake, watching the snow fall, and Logan's heart filled up. Like his arms, it overflowed. With love, happiness and hope.

* * * * *

When bull Rider Colt Mead is given temporary custody of his younger sister, he needs Jen Taylor's help. Will her growing feelings for Colt convince the ambitious cowgirl to put aside her race for glory? Find out in THE BULL RIDER'S COWGIRL, April Arrington's latest MEN OF RAINTREE RANCH *story, in stores January 2017.*

Keep reading for a sneak peek of
SUNRISE CROSSING,
the latest captivating novel in the acclaimed
RANSOM CANYON *series by*
New York Times *bestselling author*
Jodi Thomas!

CHAPTER ONE

Flight

January 2012
LAX

VICTORIA VILANIE CURLED into a ball, trying to make herself small, trying to disappear. Her black hair spread around her like a cape but couldn't protect her.

All the sounds in the airport were like drums playing in a jungle full of predators. Carts with clicking wheels rolling on pitted tiles. People shuffling and shouting and complaining. Electronic voices rattling off numbers and destinations. Babies crying. Phones ringing. Winter's late storm pounding on walls of glass.

Victoria, Tori to her few friends, might not be making a sound, but she was screaming inside.

Tears dripped off her face, and she didn't bother to wipe them away. The noise closed in around her, making her feel so lonely in the crowd of strangers.

She was twenty-four, and everyone said she was a gifted artist. Money poured in so fast it had become almost meaningless, only a number that brought no joy.

But tonight all she wanted was silence, peace, a world where she could hide out.

She scrubbed her eyes on her sleeve and felt a hand touch her shoulder like it were a bird, featherlight, landing there.

Tori turned and recognized a woman she'd seen once before. The tall blonde in her midthirties owned one of the best galleries in Dallas. Who could forget Parker Lacey's green eyes? She was a woman who had it all and knew how to handle her life. A born general who must manage her life as easily as she managed her business.

"Are you all right, Tori?" Parker asked.

Tori could say nothing but the truth. "I'm living the wrong life."

Then, the strangest thing happened. The lady with green eyes hugged her and Tori knew, for the first time in years, that someone had heard her, really heard her.

CHAPTER TWO

The stone-blue days of winter

February
Dallas, Texas

PARKER LACEY SAT perfectly straight on the side of her hospital bed. Her short, sunny-blond hair combed, her makeup in place and her logical mind in control of all emotions, as always.

She'd ignored the pain in her knee, the throbbing in her leg, for months. She ignored it now.

She'd been poked and examined all day, and now all that remained before the curtain fell on her life was for some doctor she barely knew to tell her just how long she had left to live. A month. Six months. If she was lucky, a year?

Her mother had died when Parker was ten. Breast cancer at thirty-one. Her father died eight years later. Lung cancer at thirty-nine. Neither parent had made it to their fortieth birthday.

Longevity simply didn't run in Parker's family. She'd known it and worried about dying all her adult life, and at thirty-seven, she realized her number would come up soon. Only she'd been smarter than all her ancestors. She would leave no offspring. There would be no next generation of Laceys. She was the last in her family.

There were also no lovers, or close friends, she thought. Her funeral would be small.

The beep of her cell phone interrupted her morbid thoughts.

"Hello, Parker speaking," she said.

"I'm in!" came a soft voice. "I followed the map. It was just a few miles from where the bus stopped. The house is perfect, and your housekeeper delivered more groceries than I'll be able to eat in a year. And, Parker, you were right. This isolated place will be heaven."

Parker forgot her problems. She could worry about dying later. Right now, she had to help one of her artists. "Tori, are you sure you weren't followed?"

"Yes. I did it just the way you suggested. Kept my head down. Dressed like a boy. Switched buses twice. One bus driver even told me to 'Hurry along, kid.'"

"Good. No one will probably connect me with you and no one knows I own a place in Crossroads. Stay there. You'll be safe. You'll have time to relax and think."

"They'll question you when they realize I've vanished," Tori said. "My stepfather won't just let me disappear. I'm worth too much money to him."

Parker laughed, trying to sound reassuring. "Of course, people will ask how well we know one another. I'll say I'm proud to show your work in my gallery and that we've only met a few times at gallery openings." Both facts were true. "Besides, it's no crime to vanish, Tori. You are an adult."

Victoria Vilanie was silent on the other end. She'd told Parker that she'd been on a manic roller coaster for months. The ride had left her fragile, almost shattered. Since she'd been thirteen and been "discovered" by the art community, her stepfather had quit his job and become her handler.

"Tori," Parker whispered into the phone. "You're not the tiger in a circus. You'll be fine. You can stand on your own. There are professionals who will help you handle your career without trying to run your life."

"I know. It's just a little frightening."

"It's all right, Tori. You're safe. You don't have to face the reporters. You don't have to answer any questions." Parker hesitated. "I'll come if you need me."

"I'd like that."

No one would ever believe that Parker would stick her neck out so far to help a woman she barely knew. Maybe she and Tori had each recognized a fellow loner, or maybe it was just time in her life that she did something different, something kind.

"No matter what happens," Tori whispered, "I want to thank you. You've saved my life. I think if I'd had to go another week, I might have shattered into a million pieces."

Parker wanted to say that she doubted it was that serious, but she wasn't sure the little artist wasn't right. "Stay safe. Don't tell the couple who take care of the house anything. You're just visiting, remember? Have them pick up anything you need from town. You'll find art supplies in the attic room if you want to paint."

"Found the supplies already, but I think I just want to walk around your land and think about my life. You're right. It's time I started taking my life back."

"I'll be there as soon as I can." Parker had read every mystery she could find since she was eight. If Tori wanted to disappear, Parker should be able to figure out how to make it happen. After all, how hard could it be?

The hospital door opened.

Parker clicked off the disposable phone she'd bought at the airport a few weeks ago when she and Tori talked about how to make Tori vanish.

"Miss Parker?" A young doctor poked his head into her room. He didn't look old enough to be out of college, much less med school, but this was a teaching hospital, one of the best in the country. "I'm Dr. Brown."

"It's Miss Lacey. My first name is Parker," she said as she pushed the phone beneath her covers. Hiding it like she was hiding the gifted artist.

The kid of a doctor moved into the room. "You any kin to Quanah Parker? We get a few people in here every year descended from the great Comanche chief."

She knew what the doctor was trying to do. Establish rapport before he gave her the bad news, so she played along. "That depends. How old was he when he died?"

The doctor shrugged. "I'm not much of a history buff, but my folks stopped at every historical roadside marker in Texas and Oklahoma when I was growing up. I think the great warrior was old when he died, real old. Had six wives, I heard, when he passed peacefully in his sleep on his ranch near a town that bears his name."

"If he lived a long life, I'm probably not kin to him. And to my knowledge, I have no Native American blood, and no living relatives." By the time she'd been old enough to ask, no one around remembered why she was named Parker and she had little interest in exploring a family tree with such short branches.

"I'm so sorry." Then he grinned. "I could give you a couple of my sisters. Ever since I got out of med school they think I'm their private *dial a doc*. They even call me to ask if TV shows get it right."

"No thanks, keep your sisters." She tried to smile.

"There are times when it's good to have family around." He said, "Would you like me to call someone for you? A close friend, maybe?"

She glanced up and read all she needed to know in the young man's eyes. She was dying. He looked terrible just giving her the news. Maybe this was the first time he'd ever had to tell anyone that their days were numbered.

"How long do I have to hang around here?"

The doc checked her chart and didn't meet her gaze as he said, "An hour, maybe two. When you come back, we'll make you as comfortable here as we can but you'll need—"

She didn't give him time to list what she knew came next. She'd watched her only cousin go through bone cancer when they were in high school. First, there would be surgery on her leg. Then they wouldn't get it all and she'd have chemo. Round after round until her hair and spirit disappeared. No, she wouldn't do that. She'd take the end head-on.

The doctor broke into her thoughts. "We can give you shots in that left knee. It'll make the pain less until—"

"Okay, I'll come back when I need it," she said not wanting to give him time to talk about how she might lose her leg or her life. If she let him say the word *cancer*, she feared she might start screaming and never stop.

She knew she limped when she was tired and her knee sometimes buckled on her. Her back already hurt, and her whole left leg felt weak sometimes. The cancer must be spreading; she'd known it was there for months, but she'd kept putting off getting a checkup. Now, she knew it would only get worse. More pain. More drugs, until it finally traveled to her brain. Maybe the doctor didn't want her to hang around and suffer? Maybe the shots would knock her out. She'd feel nothing until the very end. She'd just wait for death like her cousin had. She'd visited him every day. Watching him grow weaker, watching the staff grow sadder.

Hanging around had never been her way, and it wouldn't be now.

A nurse in scrubs that were two sizes too small rushed into the room and whispered, loud enough for Parker to hear, "We've got an emergency, Doctor. Three ambulances are bringing injured in from a bad wreck. Pileup on I-35. Can you break away to help?"

The doctor flipped the chart closed. "No problem. We're finished here." He nodded to Parker. "We'll have time to talk later, Miss Parker. You've got a few options."

She nodded back, not wanting to hear the details, anyway. What did it matter? He didn't have to say the word *cancer* for her to know what was wrong.

He was gone in a blink.

The nurse's face molded into a caring mask. "What can I do to make you more comfortable? You don't need to worry, dear, I've helped a great many people go through this.

"You can hand me my clothes," Parker said as she slid off the bed. "Then you can help me leave." She was used to giving orders. She'd been doing it since she'd opened her art gallery fifteen years ago. She'd been twenty-two and thought she had forever to live.

"Oh, but…" The nurse's eyes widened as if she were a hen and one of her chickens was escaping the coop.

"No buts. I have to leave now." Parker raised her eyebrow silently, daring the nurse to question her.

Parker stripped off the hospital gown and climbed into the tailored suit she'd arrived in before dawn. The teal silk blouse and cream-colored jacket of polished wool felt wonderful against her skin compared to the rough cotton gown. Like a chameleon changing color, she shifted from patient to tall, in-control businesswoman.

The nurse began to panic again. "Is someone picking you up? Were you discharged? Has the paperwork already been completed?"

"No to the first question. I drove myself here and I'll drive myself away. And yes, I was discharged." Parker tossed her things into the huge Coach bag she'd brought in. If her days were now limited, she wanted to make every one count. "I have to do something very important. I've no time to mess with paperwork. Mail the forms to me."

Parker walked out while the nurse went for a wheelchair. Her mind checked off the things she had to do as her high heels clicked against the hallway tiles. It would take a week to get her office in order. She wanted the gallery to run smoothly while she was gone.

She planned to help a friend, see the colors of life and have an adventure. Then, when she passed, she would have lived, if only for a few months.

Climbing into her special edition Jaguar, she gunned

the engine. She didn't plan to heed any speed-limit signs. *Caution* was no longer in her vocabulary.

The ache in her leg whispered through her body when she bent her knee, but Parker ignored it. No one had told her what to do since she entered college and no one, not even Dr. Brown, would set rules now.

Western Romance

Available October 4, 2016

#1613 THE BULL RIDER'S REDEMPTION
Angel Crossing, Arizona • by Heidi Hormel
Easygoing Danny Leigh is squaring off with ex-girlfriend and current nemesis Clover Van Camp. She wants to turn his beloved town into a tacky tourist resort. Can this bull-riding mayor save Angel Crossing—and win Clover back?

#1614 THE COWBOY AND THE BABY
Forever, Texas • by Marie Ferrarella
After helping Devon Bennet deliver her baby, Cody McCullough decides the pretty artist and her daughter need him. But first, this rancher turned deputy must break down the defensive walls she's built around her heart.

#1615 RESCUING THE COWBOY
Mustang Valley • by Cathy McDavid
When wrongfully imprisoned Quinn Crenshaw is finally freed, he arrives in Mustang Valley with hopes of rebuilding his life. Is single mom Summer Goodwyn willing to take a risk on a man with his past?

#1616 THE COWBOY TAKES A WIFE
Blue Falls, Texas • by Trish Milburn
Cole Davis has been married and divorced twice, so he's gun-shy about commitment. To avoid their matchmaking mothers, he and Devon Newberry "fake date." But soon Cole wonders if the third time could be the charm.

REQUEST YOUR FREE BOOKS!
2 FREE NOVELS PLUS 2 FREE GIFTS!

♦ HARLEQUIN®

Western Romance

ROMANCE THE ALL-AMERICAN WAY!

YES! Please send me 2 FREE Harlequin® Western Romance novels and my 2 FREE gifts (gifts are worth about $10). After receiving them, if I don't wish to receive any more books, I can return the shipping statement marked "cancel." If I don't cancel, I will receive 4 brand-new novels every month and be billed just $4.74 per book in the U.S. or $5.49 per book in Canada. That's a savings of at least 12% off the cover price! It's quite a bargain! Shipping and handling is just 50¢ per book in the U.S. and 75¢ per book in Canada.* I understand that accepting the 2 free books and gifts places me under no obligation to buy anything. I can always return a shipment and cancel at any time. Even if I never buy another book, the two free books and gifts are mine to keep forever.

154/354 HDN GJ5V

Name _____ (PLEASE PRINT) _____

Address _____ Apt. # _____

City _____ State/Prov. _____ Zip/Postal Code _____

Signature (if under 18, a parent or guardian must sign) _____

Mail to the **Reader Service:**
IN U.S.A.: P.O. Box 1867, Buffalo, NY 14240-1867
IN CANADA: P.O. Box 609, Fort Erie, Ontario L2A 5X3

Want to try two free books from another line?
Call 1-800-873-8635 or visit www.ReaderService.com.

* Terms and prices subject to change without notice. Prices do not include applicable taxes. Sales tax applicable in N.Y. Canadian residents will be charged applicable taxes. Offer not valid in Quebec. This offer is limited to one order per household. Not valid for current subscribers to Harlequin Western Romance books. All orders subject to credit approval. Credit or debit balances in a customer's account(s) may be offset by any other outstanding balance owed by or to the customer. Please allow 4 to 6 weeks for delivery. Offer available while quantities last.

Your Privacy—The Reader Service is committed to protecting your privacy. Our Privacy Policy is available online at www.ReaderService.com or upon request from the Reader Service.

We make a portion of our mailing list available to reputable third parties that offer products we believe may interest you. If you prefer that we not exchange your name with third parties, or if you wish to clarify or modify your communication preferences, please visit us at www.ReaderService.com/consumerchoice or write to us at Reader Service Preference Service, P.O. Box 9062, Buffalo, NY 14240-9062. Include your complete name and address.

HWR16

*Danny Leigh and Clover Van Camp have very different
ideas about how to revitalize Angel Crossing, Arizona.
But this isn't the first time the two of them have
tangled…*

*Read on for a preview of
THE BULL RIDER'S REDEMPTION,
the next book in Heidi Hormel's miniseries
ANGEL CROSSING, ARIZONA.*

"Clover?"

She turned and smiled, her perpetually red lips looking
as lush and kissable as they had been on that rodeo summer.
The one where Danny had won his buckle, lassoed a beauty
queen and lost his virginity.

"Hello, Danny," she said, a light drawl in her voice. "I
heard you were mayor of Angel Crossing. Congratulations."
She smiled again.

"Why did you buy those properties out from under
me?" he asked.

"Good investment." She turned back to the paperwork.

Danny wouldn't be dismissed. He wanted Angel
Crossing to thrive and he had plans for those properties.
He didn't want any of that to be ruined. Crossing his arms
over his chest, he stared at her…hat—not her jean-clad
rear and long legs.

Slowly, deliberately, she put down the pen and took the
papers before facing him. "What did you need, Danny?"

"I would like to know your plans for the properties, strictly as an official of the town."

"I don't think so." She looked him in the eye, nearly his height in her impractical pink cowgirl boots, matched to her cowgirl shirt. She looked the same, yet different. A woman grown into and comfortable with her blue-blood nose and creamy Southern-belle skin.

"There must be some reason you won't share your plans."

"It's business, Danny. That's all. It was nice to see you." She turned from him before he could say anything else and he watched her walk away. A beautiful sight, as it always had been. Tall, curvier than she'd been at eighteen and proud.

Now, though, what she was up to was important to him. To Angel Crossing, too. If she wouldn't tell him what she was up to, he'd find out on his own. He wasn't the big dumb cowboy who was led around by his gonads anymore. He was a responsible adult who had a town to look after…

Don't miss
THE BULL RIDER'S REDEMPTION
by Heidi Hormel, available October 2016 wherever
Harlequin® Western Romance®
books and ebooks are sold.

www.Harlequin.com

HWREXP0916

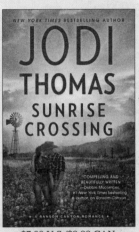

HARLEQUIN®

A *Romance* FOR EVERY MOOD™

JUST CAN'T GET ENOUGH?

Join our social communities
and talk to us online.

You will have access to the latest
news on upcoming titles and special
promotions, but most importantly,
you can talk to other fans about your
favorite Harlequin reads.

Harlequin.com/Community

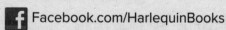

Facebook.com/HarlequinBooks

Twitter.com/HarlequinBooks

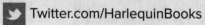

Pinterest.com/HarlequinBooks